The Case of
the Somerville
Secret

The Case of the Somerville Secret

by *Robert Newman*

Atheneum *1981* *New York*

LIBRARY OF CONGRESS CATALOGING IN PUBLICATION DATA

Newman, Robert, date
The case of the Somerville secret.

SUMMARY: Andrew and Sara help an inspector from Scotland
Yard uncover the identity of a murderer and a monster
associated with Lord Sommerville, an Assyriologist.
[1. Mystery and detective stories]   I. Title.
PZ7.N4857Case   [Fic]   80-18584
ISBN 0-689-30825-6

Published simultaneously in Canada by
McClelland & Stewart, Ltd.
Manufactured by
R. R. Donnelley & Sons, Crawfordsville, Indiana
Designed by M. M. Ahern
First Edition

Contents

1. The Man with the Yellow Eyes — 3
2. The Dead Dog — 17
3. The First Murder — 28
4. Severn Found — 49
5. The Barred Windows — 62
6. Looking for Pierre — 86
7. The Second Murder — 97
8. The False Clue — 105
9. The Encounter on the Bridge — 111
10. The Somerville Secret — 122
11. Pierre's Story — 135
12. The Monster at Large — 149
13. The Truth at Last — 162

The Case of
the Somerville
Secret

1

The Man with the Yellow Eyes

"Will you be doing anything interesting over the holiday, Chadwick?"

"Not really. I'm going to Paris."

"And you don't consider that interesting?"

"Well, I've been there before. My family's there."

"Well, this is a nice time to go—chestnuts in blossom and all that. And it should be good for your French."

"Yes, sir."

They were walking back to school after cricket; Andrew, Chadwick and Ferguson, the new language master who was coaching the house team.

"What about you, Tillett? What will you be doing?"

"Nothing very much, sir. Staying in London."

"Where he'll solve a few crimes," murmured Chadwick. "Possibly even some murders."

Ferguson started to laugh, then paused. "Wait a minute. Is your mother Verna Tillett, the actress?"

"Yes, sir."

"It seems to me I read about something happening to her last summer. Wasn't she robbed?"

"Of a famous diamond necklace," said Chadwick. "Tillett was in the middle of the whole thing, helped solve the mystery and was along on the chase when they got the jewels back."

"I wouldn't say I helped solve the mystery."

"But you were involved?" asked Ferguson.

"In a way, I suppose I was."

Andrew was thinking about that exchange now, several days later, as he walked up the Embankment toward Scotland Yard. He hadn't told Chadwick, hadn't told anyone at school, what had happened during the summer holiday, hadn't realized that anyone knew about it. But it was clear that Chadwick not only knew, but was a little jealous of Andrew. Because, in spite of his offhand, half joking manner, there had been an undercurrent of envy in what he had said. And Andrew had to admit that he didn't blame him for being envious. Because most of what Chadwick had said was true, making the time after the robbery one of the most exciting times of Andrew's life. And of course it was because of what had happened then that he was now on his way to Scotland Yard to visit Peter Wyatt, who had been a constable in the Metropolitan Police then and was now an inspector in the C.I.D.

Andrew had walked up the Thames side of the Embankment so he could watch the boats in the river. Now, waiting to cross the road, he looked at the Yard. Even if he had not known it for what it was—the headquarters of the greatest police organization in the world—he would have found the large, baronial building impressive.

A line from *The Mikado,* one of Gilbert and Sullivan's recent operettas, came to him: "To make the punishment fit the crime." He couldn't imagine why, what that had to do with the Yard, until he remembered something that Wyatt had told him the last time he had seen him; that the stone used to build the Yard was Dartmoor granite, cut and dressed by the very convicts that the Yard had helped send to hard labor at Dartmoor.

Too impatient to wait any longer for a break in the stream of traffic, he cut in behind a hansom cab, ducked under the noses of the horses drawing an omnibus, and reached the other side of the road. He went through the stone and brick archway that faced the Thames, crossed the courtyard and entered the building. After identifying himself to the desk sergeant, he was directed up a flight of stairs and along several corridors. He knocked at a numbered door, was told to come in, and then he was shaking hands with Wyatt in an office that was just big enough for a desk, a file cabinet and two chairs.

"Where's Sara?" asked Wyatt.

"At dancing school."

"During the Easter holidays?"

"They're giving two performances tomorrow, and she had to rehearse."

"Did she know that you were coming here today?"

"No. When I heard about the rehearsal, realized she couldn't come, I decided not to say anything about it."

Wyatt looked at him thoughtfully. He knew what good friends Sara and Andrew were, but he also knew about Sara's temper.

"That was sensible," he said. "But it might be dangerous. Won't she be angry?"

"She may be."

"Well, if she is, you can bring her here some other time. How's your mother?"

"Fine. At least she was when I last heard from her. She's on tour, won't be back for about ten days."

"Give her my regards when you write to her."

"I will." He studied Wyatt for a moment, comparing the way he was dressed—the well-cut, dark suit and carefully knotted tie—with the costume of the only other member of Scotland Yard he had met. "I must say that you don't look much like an inspector," he said.

"What is an inspector supposed to look like—an off-duty policeman with thick soles to his boots? Or perhaps like Finch with that horrible hat of his?"

"You're right. An inspector can look like anything. Are you on any cases now?"

"Several."

"Any interesting ones?"

"They're all interesting. What you mean is, are any of them big or important? And the answer to that is, you never know. What may seem to be very minor—a few cases of shoplifting on Bond Street—may turn out to be very major indeed." Then, as Andrew nodded, "Now I suppose you'd like me to show you around."

"Yes, I would."

"Come along then."

During the next hour Wyatt gave him a quick tour of the Yard, showing him the laboratory, the central records office, the rear entrance where informers could come in to talk to police officers without being seen by anyone else and, most interesting of all, the Black Museum. Though Andrew had heard about it, he was not quite sure what it was. It turned out to be a collection of weapons used in famous murders, burglar's tools, forgers equipment and anything else in the many categories of crime that it might be instructive for a detective to know about as part of his training. For, as Wyatt told him, there is very little new under the sun and the tricks or devices of criminals today are only variations of ones used in the past.

Wyatt looked at his watch when they left the museum and said, "Ten after five. Are you going home?"

"Yes."

"I'll drop you."

"You needn't bother. I'll take the bus."

"It's no bother. I've rooms on Gloucester Place now, so it's on my way."

They went out the rear exit to Whitehall where Wyatt hailed a hansom, and a few minutes later they were bowling north and west toward Regent's Park and St. John's Wood.

Sitting there in the swaying hansom, Andrew glanced at Wyatt and, noticing it, Wyatt said, "Why the look?"

"No reason."

"None of that now. There's a reason for everything."

"Well, I suppose it's because I thought about you quite a lot while I was at school, wondered if I'd see you again."

"Why did you wonder? I told you to let me know when you were coming back to London."

"Yes, I know, but . . . I suppose I thought you might be too busy to see me."

There was more to it than that, of course. While there was no mystery about why he felt as he did about Wyatt—what boy, even someone like Chadwick, wouldn't find him fascinating?—he was not sure he understood why Wyatt was interested in him.

"Anyone who's too busy to see his friends," said Wyatt, "doesn't deserve to have any."

He spoke, as he usually did, as directly as he would

to an equal. And Andrew suddenly had the answer to his unspoken question. For while he, Andrew, might not have a father, Wyatt had been cut off—not only from his family, but from his friends too. For police work was not anything a gentleman went in for. And therefore Andrew—and Sara—did mean a good deal to him.

Their eyes met. Then, looking away, Andrew asked about Baron Beasley, a dealer in antiques and oddities who had been very helpful to Wyatt when he was investigating the theft of the Denham diamonds, and Wyatt said he saw him fairly frequently. This led to a more detailed discussion of some of the cases he was on, and he was telling Andrew about one in particular when he suddenly sat up, rapped on the overhead trapdoor of the hansom and ordered the driver to pull up. Then, leaning forward, he called, "Polk! Sergeant Polk!"

A square-shouldered man with a closely cropped mustache who was about to enter a pub turned sharply, glanced into the hansom and said, "Mr. Wyatt. It's never you, sir!"

"But it is. Going in there?" He nodded toward the pub.

"Yes, sir."

"We'll join you. At least . . ." He glanced at Andrew. "It's just a short walk to your house. Would you like to come in with us? Or would you rather go home."

"I'd like to come with you."

"Good." Opening the leather half-door of the hansom, he got out and Andrew followed him. As Wyatt paid the cabby, Andrew looked at Polk. Though he had on a bowler and was dressed like a butler or a valet on his afternoon off in a dark grey suit, there was something unmistakably military about the way he carried himself.

"Now then," said Wyatt as the cabby touched his hat, and drove off, "my young friend here is Andrew Tillett. And this, my not-quite-so-young-friend, is Sergeant Major Polk."

"Sergeant Major," said Andrew.

"Pleased to meet you, Mr. Tillett," said Polk. Andrew now saw that his hair was grey and realized that he must be well into his sixties. But his eyes were clear and his grip when they shook hands was firm.

"As you've probably gathered," said Wyatt to Andrew, "the sergeant major was with my father's regiment; he taught me everything I know about riding and shooting."

"Not true," said Polk. "Not with the general for a father and those two brothers of yours to take you in hand."

"Then let's say you taught me things no one else did, things I'll never forget. But let's go in and celebrate this properly. A pint for you?" he asked as he ushered them into the pub.

"Yes, Mr. Wyatt."

"Get a table, and I'll be with you in a minute."

Though the pub was starting to fill up, they found a table in the corner and sat down.

"How long is it since you've seen Mr. Wyatt?" asked Andrew.

"Let's see," said Polk. "It was just before he went up to Cambridge. Must be six or seven years."

Wyatt returned with tankards of beer for Polk and himself and a bottle of ginger beer for Andrew.

"Cheers," said Wyatt, raising his tankard. "You look fit as ever, Polk."

"So do you, sir. Though I must say you don't look quite the way I thought you would."

"How do you mean?"

"Well, I heard you were with the police—a constable."

"Oh, that. Who did you hear it from—my father?"

"Yes. He was right upset about it."

"I know he was. A disgrace to the family. Well, I'm still with the police, but not in uniform. I'm an inspector in the C.I.D."

"Oh. Well, he must be pleased about that."

"I doubt it. I don't think I could do anything that would please him once I refused to go to Sandhurst."

"That *was* a disappointment to him."

"When he already had two sons in the army? But let's not go on about that. Tell me about yourself and what you're up to."

"Well, as you've probably gathered, I've retired."

"Once father did, I suspected you would. He always

said he couldn't run the regiment without you, and I didn't think you'd want to continue under anyone else."

"Well, I stayed on for another six months—Colonel Farnum asked me if I would. That took me to the end of my time—forty years in Her Majesty's uniform."

"You certainly don't look it. But what are you doing now?"

For the first time, Polk hesitated. "I . . . Well, I guess I'm what you might call a caretaker."

"Of what?"

"I'm sorry, Mr. Wyatt, but I'm afraid I can't tell you."

"Oh. Well, will you tell me where you're living, then? How can I reach you if I want to get in touch with you?"

"You can leave a message with Jem, the landlord here," he said, nodding toward the crowded bar. "He'll see that I get it."

"Righto. I'm sure you know I'm not trying to pry, Sergeant. It's just . . ." He broke off as Polk stiffened, staring across the pub. "What is it, man?"

"Nothing," said Polk. "Excuse me." He got up and made his way toward the bar. A heavyset man in rather flashy clothes had just come in and apparently ordered a beer, for the landlord was handing him a tankard. His hair was dark and, perhaps because he wore it so long or perhaps because he was so swarthy, there was something gypsy-looking about him. He turned when Polk reached him, and Andrew saw that he had yellow eyes and a scar on his cheek that ran from the corner of his eye to his chin. It must have been fairly recent for it was still red and angry looking.

Polk said something to him, and he answered briefly, started to turn back to the bar but Polk took him by the arm and pulled him around again. Pushing away, he went into a slight crouch that was so menacing Andrew would not have been surprised to see him whip out a knife. Polk seemed to expect that too, for he stepped back and raised his fists, prepared to defend himself. But now the landlord hurried over, spoke forcefully to both men. They continued to confront one another for a moment, then the scar-faced man shrugged and turned back toward the bar, and Polk turned the other way and came back toward Andrew and Wyatt. He was still quietly furious when he reached them.

"Are you all right?" Wyatt asked him.

"Yes, sir." He hesitated a moment. "What's a blodger?"

"It's Australian slang, not very complimentary."

"That's what I thought." He looked toward the bar and the scar-faced man grinned at him, raising his tank-ard mockingly. Polk was still standing and as he started back toward the bar, Wyatt put his hand on his arm.

"Steady on, Sergeant. That's a rum customer."

"That he is—even more rum than you think."

"Who is he?"

"Oh, just a chap I've had trouble with before." He remained on his feet, watching, as the man drained his tankard and put it down on the bar. Then, as he left the pub, Polk relaxed a bit.

"Well, he's gone now," said Wyatt. "Sit down and finish your beer."

"Thanks, but I think I'll be running along, too."

"After him?"

Polk smiled a little crookedly. "No, Mr. Wyatt. He may be a troublemaker, but I'm not." He held out his hand. "It was good to see you again, good to meet your young friend. Maybe next time we meet we'll really be able to talk."

"I hope so," said Wyatt. He watched as Polk crossed the pub, waved to the landlord who was behind the bar and left also.

"All right, Andrew," he said. "We're on a case together and we're comparing notes after an interview. What have you got to say about Polk?"

"Well, he didn't want to tell you exactly what he's doing or where he lives, but it's probably somewhere around here."

"What makes you say that?"

"He said if you want to get hold of him you can leave a message with the landlord here. That means they must know one another."

"Right. But *why* didn't he want me to know what he's doing or where? Is he up to any hanky-panky?"

"No. I don't think so."

"Why not?"

"I just don't. The way he shook hands, looked you in the eye, talked . . . he could just be a good actor, but I think he's straight, keeping quiet because he's supposed to."

"I agree. Unless he's changed a great deal—and I don't think he has—I believe him implicitly." He drained his tankard and set it down. "More ginger beer for you?"

"No thanks."

"Then perhaps we should trot along too. I'll walk you home."

This was one of London's quiet times, particularly in almost suburban St. John's Wood. The light of the setting sun was hazy and golden on the drawn blinds of the villas and neat brick houses, for this was tea time for all respectable people. And so the streets were deserted as Andrew and Wyatt left the pub and started walking toward Rysdale Road. No, not quite deserted, for a strange pair was coming toward them: a tall, cadaverous chimney sweep, and a small, thin boy. The man was wearing the uniform of his profession—a crooked, battered top hat and a long tailcoat—while the boy, his face smudged with soot, carried the brushes and a heavy bag of tools. The boy glanced at Andrew as he passed him, and it may have been because he was so small and his eyes were so large that he looked particularly lost and vulnerable.

Andrew looked back when he and Wyatt reached

the corner. The chimney sweep had paused in front of the pub and was looking around. Then someone across the street waved to him. The chimney sweep waved back, started toward him. The man across the street—the man who had been waiting for him—was the scar-faced man with the yellow eyes whose appearance in the pub had so provoked Polk.

2

The Dead Dog

"You're sure you don't want to come with us, Mrs. Wiggins?"

"No, dear. I've got too much to do this morning. I'll go to the afternoon performance. That's at four, isn't it?"

"I believe so."

Andrew saw no point in arguing with Mrs. Wiggins. He knew how seriously she took her responsibilities as housekeeper, and if she preferred to wait until the afternoon to see her daughter perform, that was that. Besides, if he and Sara were alone, he might be able to get things straightened out with her—something he hadn't been able to do so far.

Fred, the coachman, brought the landau around and stopped under the porte-cochere.

"Sara," called Mrs. Wiggins.

"All right," she said, coming slowly down the stairs.

She had left her costume at the school, but she carried her dancing shoes in a blue velvet bag.

"I'm not supposed to wish you luck, am I?" said Mrs. Wiggins.

"No."

"Then I won't." She kissed her. "I'll see you later."

"Yes, Mum."

Andrew opened the door for Sara and followed her out. Fred, who seemed to know everything that was going on, not only in the house but everywhere in St. John's Wood, glanced at her, then winked at Andrew. He waited till they were both seated in the rear of the landau, then chirruped to the horses and sent them down the driveway toward Rysdale Road.

Silence. The brooding silence of a temporarily quiescent volcano. Andrew glanced at Sara. She looked straight ahead at the silver buttons on the back of Fred's coat. They weren't just friends—he and Sara—they were good friends, but nothing like this had ever come up before and he did not know how to handle it. In his uncertainty, he approached it head on.

"Are you still angry?" he asked.

"Who says I'm angry?"

"Aren't you?"

"Well, if I am, don't you think I have good reason to be?"

"Why?"

"Inspector Wyatt's just as much my friend as yours. You had no right to go see him without me!"

"I told you how that happened."

"You didn't."

"Yes, I did. You just wouldn't listen. I wrote to him, told him when I was coming in from school and said we'd like to see him."

"We?"

"Yes, we. He wrote back saying we should come to the Yard the day after I got in. Well, when I got here I found you were going to be rehearsing then. I knew there was nothing you could do about that—you had to be at the school—so I thought I might as well keep the appointment."

"Why couldn't you have changed it so we could go together?"

"There wasn't time. I suppose I could have sent him a telegram saying you couldn't make it, but it seemed simpler to go and tell him. He was very sorry, said I should bring you there some other time."

"Tomorrow?"

"It depends on how busy he is. If not tomorrow, then Thursday or Friday."

"*Is* he busy? Is he on any cases?"

"He's on several—none as big as the diamond robbery. But, as he said, you never know what one will turn into."

"No. What was Scotland Yard like?"

"Big. Busy. Interesting." She seemed enough like herself now so that he dared ask, "Were you really angry at me for going there without you or are you worried about today?"

"A little of both."

"Why are you worried?"

She shrugged. "I don't know. I have two solo dances—a Scottish sword dance and a sailor's hornpipe. I'm the only one who has two."

"Well, Miss Fizdale wouldn't have you doing two if she didn't think you were good. You're going to be fine."

"We'll see." There was a small crowd gathered in front of a villa ahead of them. "What do you think's going on there?"

"I don't know." As they drew abreast of the villa, Andrew saw that there was a policeman at the center of the crowd. And, frowning as he talked to him, was a soldierly-looking man with a closely cropped mustache. "Why, there's Polk!"

"Who's Polk?"

"Sergeant Major Polk—a friend of Wyatt's. He's the man talking to the policeman."

"I know him," said Fred. "The copper, I mean. Want me to find out what's up?"

"Do we have time?"

"Won't take more than a few minutes to get to the school from here."

"Then . . . yes, we'd like to know."

"Righto."

Fred pulled up, tied the reins to a hitching post, then walked back to the small knot of people in front of the villa.

"Where'd you meet Polk?" asked Sara.

Andrew told her, told her how the sergeant had resisted telling Wyatt exactly what he did or where.

"This must be either where he lives or where he's caretaker," said Sara. "He's in his shirt sleeves and the door's open."

Andrew nodded. The way Polk stood in front of the partly open door gave a strong impression that he belonged there. Andrew looked at the villa again. He had a feeling that there was something odd about it, but it took him a moment to decide what it was. The villa, which was modest in size, was built close to the street. That meant that its grounds were behind it and to the side rather than in front of it. In most cases where this was true, the grounds would be surrounded by a hedge or a low wall. But here they were surrounded by a wall that was not only higher than any that Andrew had ever seen, but had formidable iron spikes on top of it.

As Fred paused at the edge of the small crowd, Andrew saw someone else he had seen before; the tall chimney sweep in the top hat who had come looking for the scar-faced man at the pub. He was listening to what Polk had to say to the policeman, not just with casual interest, but with complete concentration.

Sara, sitting next to Andrew, stiffened.

"Look at that!" she said angrily.

Andrew turned and saw that she wasn't looking at the villa, but further up the street. There, his back to the wall, was the small boy who had been with the chimney sweep the previous night. A group of street urchins and delivery boys, some Andrew's age and some older, surrounded him. And though most of them were grinning, the grins were not friendly. As Sara and Andrew watched, the biggest of them, a boy carrying a butcher's basket, put it down and took hold of the small boy's broom. The boy tried to hold on to it, but the butcher boy pushed him back against the wall, pulled the broom away from him and threw it out into the street.

"The bullying sods!" said Sara. She jumped out of the carriage, a fury in white muslin, and ran up the street. "Stop that!" she said, her eyes blazing. "Leave him alone!"

"Eh?" said the butcher's boy. "Wotcher mean?"

"I mean leave him alone! Why are you after him anyway?"

" 'Cause he's a bleeding Frog, that's why! Can't even speak English."

"What of it?"

"I don't like Frogs!"

"He probably doesn't like you," said Andrew who had joined Sara. "I don't myself."

"What?" The butcher's boy stared at him. "Who the devil are you two anyway?"

"I know who they are," said a hulking stable boy. "They live at twenty-three Rysdale Road. Her mum's the housekeeper there and his is a actress."

"So," said the butcher's boy, "just because you think your ma's something . . ."

"My mother's got nothing to do with it!" said Andrew angrily. "Sara told you to leave him alone. And now I'm telling you.

"Think you can make me?"

"I know I can," said Andrew. He pulled off his jacket and handed it to Sara. "Hold this."

"You mean you want to fight?" He laughed. "That's a good one!"

"Bash him, Len!" said the stable boy. "Bash him proper!"

"I'll bash him all right," said the butcher's boy as he advanced, grinning.

He was older than Andrew, probably around sixteen, taller and heavier, but from the way he put up his fists, Andrew did not think he was much of a boxer. Andrew, on the other hand, had learned old-style, bare-fisted fighting from a blacksmith in Cornwall and had continued at school.

The butcher's boy feinted two or three jabs with his left, then swung a clumsy but powerful right to Andrew's head. Andrew ducked. He knew he should fight defensively for a while, tire his opponent out, but he was too angry for caution and besides, with that wild swing, the butcher's boy had left himself wide open. Stepping in close, Andrew hit him a hard one-two just under the rib cage, knocking the wind out of him. He staggered, went down on one knee.

"Why, you . . ." he gasped. He turned slightly, caught the stable boy's eye and jerked his head.

"Righto, Len," said the stable boy. But as he started forward to join his pal, the butt end of a whip dropped down in front of his face.

"Nah, nah," said Fred. "Fair play's a jewel. One at a time—either one of you—is sporting. But two to one, and I'll take a hand."

The two boys looked at Andrew, then at Fred. He had been a jockey and he was a small man, no taller than Andrew, but he seemed very sure of himself as he stood there in his shiny boots and top hat, and he held the whip short and reversed as if he was anxious to use the loaded butt.

"Yah!" said the butcher's boy, getting to his feet. "Come on, Alf."

He picked up his basket and went off up the street, and the other boys followed him.

"Thanks, Fred," said Andrew.

"Nothing to thank me for. You were doing fine. But what was it about?"

"They were after him," said Sara, nodding toward the small, dirty-faced boy who had run out into the street to retrieve his broom.

"Why?"

"I'm not sure," said Andrew. He turned to the boy who had come back and was looking at him with large, dark eyes. "*Êtes-vous Français?*"

The boy's face lit up. "*Oui. Vous parlez Français?*"

"*Un petit peu.*"

"*Puis je vous remercie mille fois. Vous êtes mes chères amis!*"

"What's he saying?" asked Sara.

"He *is* French. That's why they were going for him," he explained to Fred. "They said he couldn't speak English—as if that was a crime. He thanked us and said we were his friends."

"Well, we are," said Sara, looking at him with sympathy and interest. "What's his name and what's he doing here?"

"My name ees Pierre," said the boy with a decided French accent.

"Then you do speak English," said Andrew.

"A leetle. Not so much as you spik French. How I come here *est vraiment une histoire.*"

"A long story," said Andrew.

"*Oui.* I come from Marseilles. You know Marseilles?"

"So there you are, ye limb," said a harsh voice. "What were you trying to do, sneak off?"

They turned. It was the cadaverous chimney sweep in the battered top hat.

"No, *m'sieu*," said Pierre anxiously. "No, no."

"Well, you better not." He looked suspiciously at Sara, Andrew and Fred. "Come on, now. We got work to do."

"*Oui, m'sieu.*" He picked up the large broom and the heavy bag with tools and brushes sticking out of it. "*Vous demeurez à vingt-trois* Rysdale Road?" he said under his breath to Andrew.

"*Oui.*"

"What are you saying, you little devil?" asked the sweep.

"Nothing, *m'sieu*."

"You're a liar, but come on." And taking him by the neck, he pulled him away and started driving him up the street, a small, slight figure with the broom over his shoulder, stooping under the weight of the heavy bag.

"Now there's someone I'd like to take the butt end of my whip to," said Fred, looking after the sweep. "What *did* the little tyke say?"

"He wanted to know if we did live at twenty-three Rysdale Road, and I said yes."

"He'd probably like to see us again," said Sara. "And I'd like to see him, find out how he got here."

"Well, there's not much chance of that," said Fred. "Not if that scabby sweep's got anything to say about it. Now do you want to know what I found out or not?"

"Yes, of course," said Andrew.

"Well, first of all, the house belongs to a real nob, Lord Somerville. He's not here right now because he's a Syri-something, a bloke who goes around digging up tombs and things."

"An Egyptologist?" asked Andrew.

"I didn't say Egypt. I said Syri-something. Anyway, like I said, he's not here now. He's somewhere in the East, like Bagdad."

"But why was the copper there?" asked Sara.

"Because their dog was killed last night."

"Whose dog?" asked Andrew.

"I guess Lord Somerville's," said Fred. "Your friend Polk said it had come from his country place in Ansley Cross."

"Was it a valuable dog?" asked Sara.

"It must have been. The constable said that Polk and the housekeeper here were real upset about it."

"How was it killed?" asked Andrew.

"The constable wasn't sure, but he thinks it was poisoned. He only got a quick look at it, but he said it was a real brute—as big as a pony."

"In other words, a watchdog," said Andrew.

"I suppose. Now if you're through protecting the weak and detecting crime, shall we proceed to the dancing school?"

"Oh, my aunt, I almost forgot about that," said Sara. "Yes, we'd better."

3

The First Murder

In spite of Andrew's best efforts, Sara did not get to Scotland Yard until the following week. He wrote to Wyatt immediately, telling him how disappointed Sara had been and how anxious she was to see him again but, as Wyatt explained later, there had been some important developments on one of his cases and it was not until the following Monday that he sent Andrew a telegram telling him to bring Sara to the Yard on Tuesday and he would take them both out to lunch.

Sara was in a very good mood—she had been ever since the dance recital at the school where she had done splendidly, as Andrew had known she would—and she enjoyed the tour of the Yard thoroughly. She was a little disappointed in the Black Museum—she had apparently expected to find wax effigies of famous criminals there like those Madame Tussaud's—but this was more than compensated for when they saw a villainous looking man with handcuffs on being brought in by two constables.

Wyatt took them to a chop house on the Strand for lunch, and it was not until they were having dessert that Andrew had a chance to bring up something that had been on his mind.

"By the way," he said, "I can tell you where you can reach your friend, Sergeant Polk."

"Where?"

"At Lord Somerville's, sixty-two Alder Road. That's apparently where he's caretaker."

"How do you know?"

Andrew told him how they had seen Polk talking to the constable on the day of Sara's recital.

"That's interesting," said Wyatt. "Is that Somerville the Assyriologist?"

"I think so," said Andrew. "Fred said he was a Syri-something."

"What's an Assyriologist?" asked Sara.

"He studies the civilizations of Assyria, Babylonia and Chaldea the way an Egyptologist studies the civilization of ancient Egypt. What was Polk talking to the constable about?"

"Their dog had been killed the night before."

"Their dog?"

"Yes. Apparently a watchdog that had been brought in from Somerville's country place."

"How was it killed?"

"The constable hadn't had a chance to go into it when Fred talked to him, but he thought it had been poisoned."

"I see."

Andrew hadn't told Sara he was going to tell Wyatt about seeing Polk—as a matter of fact, he hadn't really thought about it until that morning. But now, after a quick glance at him, Sara said, "Who do you think could have killed the dog? And why?"

"I've no idea," said Wyatt. "Maybe he howled or barked at night and that annoyed someone."

"In other words, you think one of the neighbors did it," said Andrew.

"I said I had no idea who had done it or why," said Wyatt. He looked first at Andrew then at Sara. "What are you trying to do, get me involved in another case?"

"Of course not," said Andrew, coloring guiltily. "I just thought you'd be interested because of your friend Polk."

"I am interested. And I think killing a dog is a dastardly crime. But I also think it's something the local police can handle without the assistance of the C.I.D."

"Probably," said Andrew. "You're right."

Wyatt may have been right at the time he made the statement, but by the next morning the situation had changed completely. Andrew heard about the new development just as he was finishing breakfast. He was putting some jam on his toast when, without even a perfunctory knock, the dining room door opened and Sara came in.

"Good morning," he said. Then, taking note of her seriousness, "What's up?"

"I don't know. Fred's got some kind of news but he wouldn't tell me what it was until he could tell you too."

"Oh." Then as the coachman came in, trying to look offhand, "What is it, Fred?"

"You and your holidays," said Fred. "Things are nice and quiet around here while you're away. But the minute you come back, there's trouble."

"What kind of trouble?"

"Murder."

"What?" Andrew's reaction was all that Fred could have hoped for. "Who was murdered, where and when?"

"I just heard about it, but it must have happened late last night or early this morning. And it happened at that place we stopped at the other day, Lord Somerville's on Alder Road."

"Who was murdered?" asked Sara.

"I'm not sure but I think that chap Master Andrew said he knew, that feisty caretaker."

"Polk?"

"I think so."

Murder, a frightening word and a frightening idea. But, in this case, it was not something abstract. He had met the man who had been killed, talked to him, liked him. That made it more real and more shocking. And if he—Andrew—felt that way about it, how would Wyatt, who was an old and good friend of Polk, feel?

"How did you hear about it?" he asked Fred.

"Saw the crowd when I went out to order some feed for the horses and asked the constable on point duty, the chap I know. He said Scotland Yard was coming in on it."

Sara and Andrew exchanged glances, then Andrew pushed back his chair and got up.

The constable saluted as Wyatt and the sergeant who was with him pushed their way through the crowd. They both nodded, and Wyatt knocked on the door of number 62, then said, "I don't suppose there's anything we can do about these people."

"I'm afraid not, sir," said the constable. "Not unless we clear the street. And that'll take more men than we have here right now."

"Not worth while. Word does get around, doesn't it?"

"Yes, sir."

Wyatt turned back as the door opened. A tall, somewhat stoop-shouldered man in a Norfolk jacket stood there. He was probably in his forties, but it was hard to be sure for though his hair was only touched with grey, his face was drawn and deeply lined.

"Good morning. I'm Inspector Wyatt of Scotland Yard."

"I've been expecting you—you or someone. I'm Somerville."

"Oh. How do you do, sir. Forgive me if I seem surprised. I heard you were away."

"I was, but I returned to London at the end of last week."

"I see." Then, indicating the big man who was with him, "This is Sergeant Tucker of the Wellington Road police station. He'll be working with me on this case."

"Sergeant." Somerville nodded to Tucker.

"My lord . . ."

"Please come in." Though it was clear that he was very distressed, Somerville was doing his best to observe the amenities. "I know you want to talk to me about what happened last night, but there's someone else you should talk to as well. She's in here."

He opened a door to the right of the entrance hall, motioned them in. They found themselves in a small, simply furnished parlor. Sitting in a straight-backed chair on the far side of the room was a middle-aged woman with strong, rather craggy features and piercing eyes. She had on a plain, dark dress and her hair was pulled back severely. She sat very erect and was quite pale, but that may have been because she was in pain, for she had an ugly bruise on her forehead, a cut over her eye and her right arm was bandaged and in a sling.

"This is Mrs. Severn, my housekeeper," said Somerville. "Inspector Wyatt and Sergeant Tucker."

They both bowed to her.

"I'd like to tell you how sorry I am about what happened," said Wyatt. "I should also tell you that I have a special interest in the case because I knew Sergeant Polk—knew him and liked him very much."

"Were you army, too?"

"No, but the army is the connection. He was sergeant major in my father's regiment."

"You're General Wyatt's son?"

"Yes."

"I knew he had two sons who were in the army. I didn't know he had one who was in the police."

"It's not something he talks about," said Wyatt dryly.

"I see. That explains my feeling that you were not a ordinary policeman. Does it also explain your presence on the case?"

"Probably. The superintendent saw your name on the occurrence sheet, called me in and asked me if I knew you. When I said I didn't, but did know Polk, he told me to take over."

"That makes for an interesting coincidence. Because it was your father who recommended Polk to me."

"You and Father are friends?"

"I wouldn't say that. I'm not here enough to be friends with anyone. But we're both members of the Travellers Club. And when I mentioned that I was looking for someone to keep an eye on the place while I was away, he suggested Polk."

"That was what he did, acted as caretaker?"

"Yes."

"What other help do you have here?"

"None."

"There was just Mrs. Severn and Polk? No cook or parlor maid?"

"No. I'm away most of the time, and when I'm here, my wants are very simple and Mrs. Severn is able to take care of them easily. She's been with me for a long time. About fifteen years, isn't it?" he said, looking at her.

"Sixteen this last February," she said. Her voice was rather husky, but pleasant.

"That long?" said Somerville. "Yes, I guess it is. She was with me, took care of things down at Ansley Cross before I closed the place, moved here to London."

"I see. Now will you tell us exactly what happened last night?"

"I'll try." Somerville glanced at Tucker who had seated himself unobtrusively in the corner and opened his notebook, then said suddenly, angrily, "This is awful, terrible! You say you knew Polk, liked him. But I not only knew and liked him—I feel responsible for what happened to him! If I hadn't engaged him, he'd still be alive, and . . ." He broke off. "I'm sorry, but it's been very much on my mind."

"Yes, I can see it has."

"What was it you asked me?"

"To tell us what you can about last night."

"Yes. Well, I had been here for several days and was going back to Paris. Mrs. Severn and Polk were coming with me."

"Just a second," said Wyatt. "You said you were going back to Paris?"

"Yes."

"I was under the impression that when you were away you were in the Middle East."

"Most of the time I am—in Mesopotamia. But I also spend a good deal of time in Paris. I've been doing some work with Fauré, the French Assyriologist."

"Why were you taking Mrs. Severn and Polk with you?"

"Because I expected to spend more time than ever in Paris now, and I didn't like living in a hotel. I planned to take a house and have Mrs. Severn take care of it for me."

"With Polk's help."

"I hadn't made up my mind whether I wanted Polk to stay with us in Paris or come back here. But I wanted him to make the trip with us as a protective measure."

"Protective?"

"Yes. I was taking some very valuable things back to Paris with me; some votive figures, early Kassite pottery and quite extraordinary jewelry I had dug up at Tell Iswah."

"I see. And how were you planning to travel?"

For the first time Somerville hesitated. "I'm afraid that's where I made a mistake. I was anxious about taking the train to Dover, so I arranged to have Polk drive us there."

"At night?"

"Yes. I thought we'd be safe enough at this end, and of course it would be daylight by the time we arrived at Dover. But . . ." Again he hesitated.

"Yes?"

"I had planned to leave about midnight, but it took me longer than I thought to get ready and it was after three before I helped Polk carry the chest out to the brougham.

"The chest with the valuables in it, the things you were concerned about?"

"Yes. They were in a strongbox, which we put inside the brougham. Mrs. Severn got in, too, and I came back into the house to see if I'd forgotten anything and lock up. I was in here when I heard a noise outside—a shout, the sound of several blows, and a scream. I went running out, and there was the brougham going off up the street hell for leather. I couldn't understand what had happened until I saw Mrs. Severn and Polk both lying on the pavement."

"Was Polk dead?"

"No, not yet. I looked at Mrs. Severn first. She was unconscious, but when I started to pick her up, she opened her eyes, saw Polk and told me to take care of him. I went to him. His head was bloody and he was breathing very peculiarly. Mrs. Severn got to her feet and in spite of her injuries—her wrist was broken—she helped me carry him into the house. Then I went to get a doctor."

"What doctor was that?"

"There's one, a Dr. Davison, just up the street. I've never used him, but I knew about him. I woke him, told him he was needed, and he got dressed and came back here with me. By the time we got to the house, Polk was dead."

"What did he say was the cause of death?"

"A blow on the temple with a club, or something of that sort. He said he thought the skull had been fractured."

"Our doctor is doing an autopsy, but that's his initial opinion, too. Now will you tell us what you can about the incident, Mrs. Severn?"

"Yes, Inspector. But I'm afraid I can't tell you very much."

"Why?"

"Because I'm not sure exactly what did happen. As Lord Somerville told you, I got into the brougham. Polk was with the horses, looking at their harness. He had said something about wanting to tighten one of the martingales. Suddenly I heard an exclamation and the sound of a struggle. There were several blows. As I started to open the door to see what was happening, it was opened from the outside, someone took hold of me and pulled me out, letting me fall to the ground. I put out my hand to break the fall—that's how I broke my wrist—but my head hit the ground, and that's the last thing I remember."

"Did you see the man who pulled you out?"

"No, I didn't. It all happened too quickly, and besides it was too dark."

"Can you tell us anything about him even though you couldn't see him? For instance, was it your feeling that he was tall or short or particularly strong?"

"No, I can't tell you anything about him. I think he must have been fairly strong because he pulled me out without any trouble."

"Was it your impression that there was just one man involved in the attack, or were there more than one?"

Mrs. Severn frowned. "I hadn't really thought about that—I've been too shaken up. But now that I do . . . I think there must have been more than one."

"Why do you say that?"

"Well, the door was opened at almost the same time

as poor Sergeant Polk was attacked. Whoever attacked him wouldn't have had time to come around to the door."

Wyatt nodded. "That was my impression from your description of what happened, but I wanted to make sure. Now can you tell us anything about the brougham so that we can institute a search for it?"

"I'm afraid not," said Somerville. "Polk rented it from a livery stable somewhere near the Wellington Road."

"There's just one in the neighborhood," said Tucker. "In the mews behind Marlborough Place. I know the liveryman, and I'll inquire."

"Good," said Wyatt. Then, turning to Somerville, "Is it your feeling that the brougham was taken in order to get possession of the chest that was in it?"

"I can't think of any other reason."

"Who knew about it? Knew that you had valuable antiquities and jewelry in the house here and were planning to move them to Paris?"

"Anyone who had read my monographs on the dig at Tell Iswah would know what I'd found there, and might suspect I had the items here in the house. But no one knew I was going to take them to Paris."

"No one?"

"Not that I know of."

"Do you think there could be any connection between the killing of your watchdog and this incident?"

Somerville frowned. "I never thought of that, but
. . . what connection could there be?"

"I can think of only one reason why anyone would
want to kill a watchdog, and that's because someone
wanted to enter the premises and didn't want to have to
deal with the dog or have it give the alarm."

"But no one did enter the premises. At least, I don't
think anyone did."

"Would you know?"

"Why, yes. I assume the purpose of breaking in would
be robbery, and there was no robbery—nothing was
stolen—until last night."

"Someone might have wanted to look over the place,
see if there was anything worth stealing, and decided
there was but that it would be better to wait for a more
favorable occasion." He turned to Mrs. Severn again.
"Did Sergeant Polk have anything to say about the killing of the dog?"

"Well, he was very angry about it. It was he who
called the police. But he never said why he thought it
was done."

"Do you by any chance know a dark-haired, gypsy-
looking man with yellow eyes and a scar on his cheek?"

Mrs. Severn stiffened. "Why do you ask that?"

"Because, when I ran into Polk last week and we went
into a pub near here, the man I described came in and
Polk had words with him. He told me afterwards that
it was someone he'd had trouble with before."

Mrs. Severn hesitated, looking at Somerville. "Yes. I think I know who he is," she said.

"Who?"

"My husband, Tom."

"Your husband?"

"Yes. I hadn't seen him for sixteen years, since before I went to work for his lordship down at Ansley Cross."

"Where has he been? Your husband, I mean."

"Where?" Her eyes blazed. "Where he belongs—in jail! At least, that's where he was to begin with—for ten years. After that he left the country, and I heard he'd gone to Australia."

"Why was he in jail? What was the charge?"

"Robbery and assault with a deadly weapon." Then, as Wyatt glanced at Somerville, "His lordship knew about it."

"Yes, I did," said Somerville. "He was a thoroughly unsavory and dangerous fellow. He'd been brought up several times for poaching and disturbing the peace and was finally sent away, as Mrs. Severn said, for robbery and assault."

"How did Polk know him? What was his connection with him?"

"His only connection with him was when Tom showed up here," said Mrs. Severn. "I don't know why he came back from Australia. Maybe he got in more trouble there. When he got back, he must have gone down to Ansley Cross looking for me, heard I was here in London. Anyway, the first I knew about it was when the bell rang one morning and I opened the door and there he was."

"When was this?"

"A little over a week ago."

"What did he want?"

"What he always wanted, money. That's not what he started with, of course. He began by saying he'd missed me, wanted to get together with me again. When I told him I wanted nothing to do with him, he said that, in that case, I should pay him to go away. He turned nasty when I said I wouldn't do that either, but then Polk came to the door. He'd heard enough to guess what was going on, and he told Tom if he didn't go, he'd call the police."

"And did he go?"

"Yes, he did. He said he'd be back, but Polk told him he'd better not if he knew what was good for him."

"Could it have been he who was here last night?"

"I don't know. I told you I didn't see either the man who pulled me out of the brougham or the one who attacked Polk. But I suppose it's possible."

"Do you have any idea where I can find him?"

"No, I don't. I never asked him where he was staying, and he never said."

"Right." Wyatt stood up. "You've both been very helpful, told us some interesting things. Are you still planning to go to Paris?" he asked Somerville.

"No. Not after what's happened. I shall remain here for at least the next few weeks."

"Good. Then I'll be able to reach you if there's anything more I need to know."

"I'll be here or at my club. And I assume you'll let me know if there are any developments; if you find out who killed Polk and made off with the brougham."

"Of course." Wyatt bowed to Mrs. Severn and left the room followed by Sergeant Tucker. Somerville accompanied them to the door and let them out.

The constable was still on duty, even though there were fewer people standing about and watching the house than there had been before. Among them, not gaping or staring but waiting patiently, were Sara and Andrew. Catching Wyatt's eye, they came forward.

"What are you doing here?" he asked.

"We heard what happened, and we wanted to tell you how sorry we were," said Andrew. "I know you liked Polk."

"Yes, I did," said Wyatt quietly. "What else?"

"Nothing else," said Sara. "Except that we wondered what you were going to do about lunch."

"I hadn't really thought about it. I suppose we'll go to a pub. The one I met Polk at is just around the corner, isn't it?" he asked Tucker.

"The Red Lion," said Tucker.

"Well, of course you can if you want to," said Andrew. "But we heard a sergeant was with you, and we had a feeling you'd probably want to talk to him. And we thought, if you did, you might want to come back to Rysdale Road for lunch."

"And where would you be while we were talking?" asked Wyatt.

"Why, no place," said Sara. "I mean, if you didn't want us around, we'd make ourselves scarce."

"I'm sure," said Wyatt ironically. "These are two young friends of mine," he said to Tucker. "Sara Wiggins and Andrew Tillett. Sergeant Tucker."

"How do." said Tucker, shaking hands with them. "Seems to me I've heard of them. Very helpful in the Denham diamond case, weren't they?"

"Don't think I'd have been able to solve it without them. What do you think of their offer?"

"Well, they'd give us some sort of place at The Red Lion where we could be private. But we could never be sure someone wasn't eavesdropping. Besides, the food's been a little off there lately."

"In other words, you vote for Rysdale Road. All right."

He waved to a four-wheeler that was coming up the street, gave the driver the address, and they all got in. Wyatt said nothing during the drive to the house and, after an exchange of glances, Sara and Andrew remained silent, too. Matson, the butler, let them in and showed them to the dining room. He and Mrs. Wiggins had been told that there might be company for lunch, and after

Mrs. Wiggins had greeted Wyatt and been introduced to Sergeant Tucker, lunch was served, and the four were left alone.

"Well, Sergeant," said Wyatt, helping himself to some mustard for the cold beef, "what do you think?"

"This beef looks prime, sir. Much better than we could get at The Red Lion."

"I'm sure it is. But that's not what I meant."

"No, sir." Tucker looked at Sara and Andrew who were sitting there quietly, trying to be as unobtrusive as possible. "Well, there are several things that struck me as rather odd."

"For instance?"

"Thinking it would be safer to take something valuable to Dover by carriage than by train."

"Somerville admitted that might have been a mistake."

"Yes, I know. But if he was worried, why did he travel at night?"

"He explained that, claimed he wasn't worried about anything happening at this end, but didn't want to arrive at Dover after dark."

"I know. But I still think it was very strange."

"You think he was lying?"

Tucker was silent for a moment. "I wouldn't say that, sir. I think he was very upset at what happened—about both Polk's death and the chest that was stolen—perhaps even more upset than he let on. But, at the same time, I don't believe he told us everything he knows."

"I agree with you. What about Mrs. Severn?"

"There again I had a strange feeling. I wonder if she would have told you about that no-good husband of hers coming to see her if you hadn't known about him, asked her about him."

"Well, it's not easy for a woman to admit she was foolish enough to marry a man who turned out to be a criminal. However, I agree with you again. Do you think she was lying when she said she didn't know where we could find him?"

"No, I don't. I don't think she was trying to protect him, if that's what you mean. Because one of the things I'm sure about is that she hates him."

"I don't think there's any doubt about that. And though she said she didn't know who attacked her and Polk, I'd like to have a few words with Tom Severn, find out where he was last night."

"Do you have any idea of where you might find him, sir?"

"No. But I know someone who might know."

"Your friend Beasley?"

"Yes. If you'll go back to the Yard when you've finished your lunch and check central records for anything they have on Severn, I'll go to Portobello Road and see what Beasley has to say."

Sara hadn't said a word during the discussion between Wyatt and the sergeant, but this was too much for her.

"Can we go with you?" she asked.

Wyatt looked at her with pretended surprise.

"Are you still here?"

"Yes. I asked if we could go with you."

"Why?"

"Because we like the Baron. He's almost as much of a friend as you are, and we haven't seen him for a long time."

"And that's the only reason?"

"No. We could understand a little of what happened from things you and the sergeant said. But if we go to Portobello Road with you, you'll have a chance to tell us more."

"And of course it's very important that you know everything that the sergeant and I know."

"Why, yes," said Sara with wide-eyed innocence. "Because, if we don't, how are we going to help you?"

Wyatt looked at her intently, then turned to Tucker.

"You see what I'm up against? What I've *been* up against?"

"Yes, sir," said Tucker smiling. "But it didn't do any harm in the Denham diamond case. Maybe it won't in this one either."

"We'll see."

4

Severn Found

Though Fred was available and would have been happy to drive them anywhere they wanted to go, Wyatt hailed a hansom and told the cabby to take them to Portobello Road. The reason for that was that Fred would not only have listened to everything Wyatt said, but would have commented on it as well. Without these interruptions, by the time they reached Portobello Road, Wyatt had told them everything that had happened at Lord Somerville's and had even had time to answer a few of their questions.

This was not one of Portobello Road's busy days, and the street was almost deserted as they walked up it to Beasley's shop. The window contained the same oddments it had when they visited before—a brass samovar, some glass paperweights and a marble head of Napoleon.

Beasley, a large, babyfaced man in a bottle green velvet jacket, looked at them coldly as they came in.

"So we're in trouble again, eh?" he said in his whispery, wheezing voice.

"Is that an editorial we or a royal we?" asked Wyatt.

"I don't know what that means. I'm referring to you and these two creatures, whoever they are."

"But you know who we are," said Sara. "At least, you ought to."

"If I do, it's because I've got a memory like an elephant. How long is it since you've been here?"

"A long time," said Andrew. "But I've been away at school."

"Excuses, excuses. What about you?" he asked Sara. "Have you been away at school, too?"

"No, but I didn't think I should come here by myself."

"Of course not! You can do anything you feel like doing—hooking midnight rides on criminal's wagons, for instance. But you can't come across London to see the man who helped you solve one of the century's most famous cases."

"It wasn't because I was *afraid* to come here by myself. It's because Andrew would have been furious at me. Because he would have wanted to come, too. We both missed you. And when the inspector said he was going to come and see you, we told him he just had to let us come, too."

"Sounds like a lot of Betty Martin to me. Howsomever . . . here." He produced a block of something wrapped in paper. "Have some halvah."

"What's halvah?" asked Sara as he unwrapped a white substance, took out a clasp knife and cut a slice.

"What's halvah?" he repeated unhappily. "Am I the only one who's interested in your education? First taste it and see if you like it."

He cut the slice into quarters and gave Sara and Andrew each one. It was sticky and very sweet, but very good.

"Yes," said Sara. "It's like . . . I don't know what it's like. What's it made of?"

"Crushed nuts and honey. It's Middle Eastern." He popped one of the two remaining pieces in his mouth, held the other out to Wyatt.

"Thanks," said Wyatt, taking it. "I happen to like halvah. And while I'm usually more concerned about my weight and my teeth than you are, I'll ignore that for the moment."

"There's nothing wrong with either my teeth or my weight," said Beasley. "All right. What's your problem?"

"I'm trying to find a cove named Severn. Tom Severn. Have you heard of him?"

"Not by that name. Tell me more about him."

"Well, he's an old lag, did ten years at hard, probably at Dartmoor, then went to Australia and came back fairly recently. He's in his late thirties but looks older;

tall, well set up, dark hair and rather good looking in a gypsyish way." He glanced at Andrew. "Anything to add to that?"

"He has yellow, tigerish eyes and a bad cut on his cheek, a biggish slash."

Beasley shook his head. "No. Haven't seen him. What do you want him for?"

"I'd like to ask him a few questions about a murder and robbery that took place last night on Alder Road."

"Well, I'll pass the word, but it will probably take a little time before I can get anything for you."

"I don't *have* the time. It's an important case and he's the only lead I've got. Is there anyone who might know more about him than you?"

"I can't think of anyone at the moment—at least anyone who'd talk to you. But . . . you said he had a cut on his cheek," he said to Andrew. "Was it a new one?"

"I think so. It was still pretty red and angry looking."

"Well, if he had someone take care of it, sew it up and all that . . . maybe you should talk to Doc Owen."

"Who's Doc Owen?"

"What kind of a copper are you? I thought you knew your London."

"Not every part of London. Is he around here?"

"Yes."

"I count on you to let me know about that. Tell me about him."

"Well, he's a real and rorty gent, been around here

for years. He's got a dicky leg, walks with a stick, but he's a top-hole doc. I don't know why he's here instead of over on Harley or Wimpole Streets, but this is where he is, has his surgery and dispensary just a few blocks from here, up and over toward Westbourne Park."

"Why should he know about Severn?"

"I told you why. If you go to hospital or almost any doctor with a bad cut, they'll ask you questions about it. But not Owen. He says it's none of his business and none of the police's business either. He's gotten them angry more than once for not reporting things, but they know how the people around here feel about him—if you've no money he doesn't charge you, no matter what he has to do—so they leave him alone."

"Maybe we should talk to him. He's up the road, you say?"

"Up a few blocks, then east. Ask anyone for Doc Owen, and they'll direct you."

"Right. In the meantime, you'll spread the word and let me know if you hear anything?"

"I will."

They followed Beasley's directions; and the change in the surroundings as they went, though gradual, was dramatic. London is made up of a whole series of small villages that are quite different from one another. Portobello Road, for instance, was very different from the respectability of St. John's Wood; the buildings were quite shabby, the shops crowded close to one another and the street not very clean. But Portobello Road was elegant compared to the area through which they soon walked. Even Sara, who had grown up in two tiny rooms over a livery stable off Edgeware Road, was sobered by what she saw; houses, not merely dilapidated, but in the last stages of decay, with broken windows and no doors. The children who played in the street were ragged and dirty; half of them were barefoot, and all of them looked, not only hungry, but as if they had always been hungry.

At one point, unsure of the way, Wyatt asked a thin, grey-haired woman in a shawl where they could find Dr. Owen.

"Well, one day it'll be in heaven, at the right hand of the Savior," she said with a touch of brogue, "for it's a saint he is, a blessed saint. But now he's right there, in that building straight ahead."

Though the building she pointed to needed painting, it was sounder than any around it. The three low steps had been swept, the door was solid, and next to it was a sign that said, Bruce Owen, M.D.

They went in and found themselves in a small waiting room. An old man and old woman and a young mother with an infant in her arms sat on benches against the wall. They all stared at Wyatt, Sara and Andrew.

"Were you wanting the doctor?" asked the young mother.

"Yes," said Wyatt.

"Sister Rose'll be out in a minute. You'll have to talk to her first."

"Thank you," said Wyatt. As they started to sit down, a door opened and an elderly woman wearing rimless glasses, a grey uniform, white cap and apron came out.

"Yes?"

"I'd like to see Dr. Owen if I may," said Wyatt.

"Morning office hours are over," she said firmly. "Unless it's an emergency."

"It isn't an emergency, but it is rather important," said Wyatt patiently. "I don't want to see him professionally. I merely want to talk to him for a moment."

"About what?"

Wyatt took out a card and gave it to her.

"Scotland Yard," she said, reading it. "The doctor doesn't like the police much."

"So I've heard. But I'd still like to talk to him."

She looked at him sharply.

"Wait here," she said, and went back through the door. She came out again almost immediately.

"All right. In here," she said. Then, ironically, as Sara and Andrew started to follow him, "Are they from Scotland Yard, too?"

"No. They just came here with me. Would you rather they waited outside?"

"It doesn't matter." She led them down a hall, paused in front of an open door. "Inspector Wyatt," she said, then went back to the waiting room.

A man, sitting at a desk with his back to them, turned around. He was in his late fifties, his hair was grey, and his face was lined, but he seemed alert and vigorous. Instead of the dark coat and striped trousers that were virtually a doctor's uniform, he had on a suit of rather worn tweeds.

"Good morning, Inspector," he said pleasantly. "What can I do for you?"

"There's someone I'm trying to find, someone I'd like to ask a few questions, and I thought perhaps you might be able to help me."

"Who is this person?"

"His name is Severn."

"Tom Severn?"

"Why, yes. Do you know him?"

"Yes."

"Would you also know where I can find him?"

"Of course. He's here."

"Here?"

"Yes. I'll take you to him." A heavy cane was hooked over the end of the desk, and the doctor used it to get to his feet, leaned on it as he limped toward the door. Sara and Andrew, self-conscious after Sister Rose's remark, had hung back, and Dr. Owen glanced at them curiously.

"Are these young people with you?" he asked.

"Yes."

"It's an interesting gambit, disarming and distracting. It could make people forget who you are and what you're after."

"It's not a gambit. We just happened to be visiting someone, a friend, and he suggested that you might be able to help me find Severn."

"Really? Right." He stumped on down the corridor. "Besides my surgery, I have a few beds here for patients who, for one reason or another, can't go to a hospital."

He opened a door that led into a room larger than either the waiting room or the surgery. There were half a dozen beds in it. Three were empty. An old man lay in one of the others, a three or four year old boy in a second, and in the last, the one nearest the door, was the gypsyish looking man with the yellow eyes and the slash on his cheek. His right leg was in a bulky cast that extended from the sole of his foot to his hip, all of which was raised and supported by a system of ropes and pulleys that hung from hooks in the ceiling.

"Someone here to see you, Tom," said Dr. Owen.

"Oh? Who?

"My name's Wyatt. I'm an inspector with the Metropolitan Police."

"A busy, eh?" Severn looked at him more closely. "I've seen you before."

"Yes. At The Red Lion in St. John's Wood."

57

"That's right. You were with the pukka sergeant with the ramrod up his back. What's his name—Polk?"

"Yes."

"How is the old blodger?"

"He's dead."

"What?" Severn stiffened, looked sharply at Wyatt, at the doctor, then turned back to Wyatt. "Is that what you want to talk to me about?"

"One of the things, yes."

"When did he die? And how?"

"I've answered quite a few of your questions. Do you mind if I ask you a few?"

"No."

"What's wrong with you?"

"Broken leg. Right, Doc?"

Owen, leaning on his stick in the doorway, nodded. "Compound fractures of both the tibia and the fibula."

"How did it happen?"

"I was kicked by a horse."

"Where was this?"

"Over near Paddington."

"How did it happen?"

"I was pegging a hack when the horse started limping. I got down to see if he'd picked up a stone and he lashed out at me."

"Are you a licensed cab driver?"

"No. I'm a buck."

"How did you get here?"

"One of the cabbies on the line brought me. He wanted to take me to St. Mary's, but I don't like hospitals so I said no. I knew Doc Owen—he'd stitched my face up—so I told him to bring me here."

"When was this?"

"You mean, when did it happen? Oh, about nine-thirty last night."

Wyatt turned to Owen. "Is that true, Doctor?"

"I don't know precisely when it happened, but . . . Sister Rose," he called. "Will you bring me the admissions register?"

"Yes, Doctor." She came down the hall carrying a large book bound in grey cloth. Owen took it and, leaning against the door jamb, began turning the pages. He did it rather awkwardly, and Andrew noticed that he was left-handed.

"Here we are," said Owen. "He was admitted at ten minutes after ten."

He handed the book to Wyatt, who looked at the entry he pointed to, then at the entries before and after it, then gave it back.

"Do you usually see patients that late, Doctor?"

"It's well after my regular office hours, but I live upstairs so that, in an emergency, I can be reached at any time."

"I see. Well, thank you very much, Doctor. I'm sorry to have troubled you." If Wyatt was disappointed, there was no sign of it in his manner. "You too, Severn."

"That's all right," said Severn. "Now will you tell me what happened to old Polk? And when?"

"He was struck on the head and killed a little after three o'clock in the morning."

"You mean *this* morning?"

"Yes."

Severn whistled softly. "I never expected I'd think breaking a leg was lucky, but maybe it was."

"Yes, maybe. Thank you again, Doctor."

"Not at all."

Sara and Andrew, who had been waiting just outside the open door, followed Wyatt down the corridor and through the waiting room. It was only when they were outside that the inspector's feelings became evident in his scowl and the way he walked.

"Then that's that," said Sara. "He couldn't have done it."

"Not with a double compound fracture of the leg, no."

"What's a buck?" asked Andrew.

"An unlicensed cab driver. Licensed cab drivers are allowed to hire them as substitutes for up to twenty-four hours. He can't be a licensed cabby because he's been in jail."

"Oh. What are you going to do now?"

"I don't know."

"But you must know," said Sara.

"Do you really think that's the way it happens?" he

asked, smiling painfully. "That when a lead ends no-
where, we immediately pick up another one and go off
like a pack of hounds? It isn't. All you can do, when
you're on a case, is list all the things you want to know
and start trying to find out what you can about each
of them."

"Like finding Severn."

He nodded. "Exactly. I wanted to find him and we
did, more easily than I thought we would, but that
proved to be a dead end, so now we'll have to go on to
other things."

"Like what?"

"Finding Somerville's brougham. If or when we do,
that may give us some clue as to who took it—which in
turn may tell us who killed Polk. Then I'm afraid we're
going to have to come back to Somerville himself."

"Why do you say you're afraid?" asked Andrew.

"Because it's an awkward situation. Sergeant Tucker
and I both feel that he was not completely honest with
us. That there were things he was not telling us. However I don't want to accuse him of that until I have
some idea of what it is he's hiding."

"And how will you find that out?"

"I wish I knew."

5

The Barred Windows

"Well?" asked Andrew.

It was the next morning, and he and Sara were standing under a large beech tree and looking at the Somerville house from the open ground across the street.

"There *is* something funny about it," said Sara. She frowned as she studied it. "I know! It's the wall!"

"What about it?"

"Well, the house isn't very big—it's about the same size as most of the villas around here. And the grounds aren't very big either. But the wall around it is higher than the one around Three Oaks, and the grounds there are as big as a park with a lake and greenhouses and all."

Three Oaks, home of the Marchioness of Medford and one of the largest estates in St. John's Wood, was next door to the Tillett house. Sara had said exactly what

Andrew had thought himself, but he played the devil's advocate.

"Maybe the wall around Three Oaks isn't as high because it goes on forever and it would cost a mint to make it higher."

"The wall around Three Oaks is high enough to keep anyone from looking in or getting in unless they use a ladder. No, I say there's something funny about this wall. Look at the spikes on top of it. And the broken glass."

"Well, according to Wyatt, Somerville did have some things he was worried about—jewelry and things he'd dug up in Mesopotamia."

"But he'd keep those in the house, wouldn't he? And the wall doesn't go round the house, just around the grounds." The wind tugged at her hat, and she clutched it as she looked at him sharply. "You're just trying it on with me, aren't you? Because you think there's something funny about it, too."

"Yes, I do. I'd like to get inside and see what's there. Or even just look inside."

"That's what somebody else wanted. At least, that's what Wyatt thinks—why the watchdog was killed."

"I know."

"Well, if we think there's something funny about it, Wyatt certainly must. Why doesn't he go back in and look around?"

"Perhaps he will. But it's not going to be easy for him.

Because the murder didn't take place inside the house or the grounds but outside, here in the street. And Lord Somerville didn't ask him if he wanted to look around when he was in there."

"But he can still get in if he wants to, can't he? Even if he has to get a search warrant."

"Yes, but I don't think he'll do that. As he said, he doesn't want to get into a row with Lord Somerville. He'll probably think of some very clever way of getting in."

"Like what?"

"I don't know." He had been looking around as he talked. Then, as another gust of wind shook the branches over their head, a strange expression came over his face. "Do you like kite flying?" he asked.

"I don't know. I've never done any."

"Well, this is a good day for it. Where can we buy a kite?"

"You're up to something, aren't you?"

Andrew grinned.

"I can see you are. I shouldn't help you till you tell me what it is, but . . . there's a shop on the Wellington Road that probably has kites."

"Let's go see."

The shop did have kites. Andrew bought one and a ball of twine, and they took them both back to Alder Road. The wind was rather erratic and not too strong, but he thought he could get the kite up. As Sara watched, he went to the downwind end of the open ground and, balancing the kite on the palm of his right hand, he began to run. When the kite lifted, he let it go, paying out twine. Several times the kite wavered, hesitated, but each time he was able to steady it, keep it in the air, by jerking on the line, and finally it had mounted to well above the trees and was flying steadily and pulling strongly.

"Coo! That's lovely!" said Sara. "Can I try it?"

"Of course. Here." He gave her the ball of twine.

"What do I do?"

"Let out more line if you want it to go higher. Jerk on the line if it starts to wobble or fall."

She played the kite for some time, letting out more and more line until there was almost none left on the ball.

"It's not half pulling," she said, looking up to where it flew much higher than the steeple of St. John's. "Maybe you'd better take it."

"Right." Andrew had picked up a short piece of stick and, tying the end of the twine to it, he began winding the line on to it.

"Are you bringing it down?" Sara asked.

"Yes."

"Why?"

He didn't answer but began moving slowly out toward the street on the upwind side of the large beech tree. Sara watched, a little puzzled.

"Look out!" she said finally. "If you're not careful it'll land in the tree."

Andrew jerked hard on the string, the kite swooped, then as she had predicted, dived into the topmost branches of the tree.

"Well, that did it," said Sara. "What are you going to do now?"

"I don't want to lose it," said Andrew, his face expressionless. "If Fred gave me a hand with a ladder, I think I could climb up and get it."

Frowning, Sara looked at him, at the tree, then across the road at the Somerville house.

"Well, aren't you Roger, the artful dodger," she said admiringly.

"It's worth a try, don't you think?"

"Yes, I do."

"Will Fred give us any trouble?"

"If he does, I'll give him some. Come on." But, as Andrew dropped the ball of twine at the foot of the tree. "Wait a bit. Maybe we won't need Fred."

He turned. Wyatt, not looking very happy, was coming down Alder Road toward them. Sergeant Tucker was with him.

"Hello, you two," he said. "What are you doing here?"

"We were flying a kite," said Sara, "and it dived into the top of that tree." She looked at him with a significant eye. "Do you think the sergeant could give Andrew a leg up? If he did, Andrew thinks he could probably climb the tree and get it."

Wyatt frowned, not in puzzlement as Sara had, but with impatience.

"Now look," he said, "fun's fun, but . . ." The steadiness of her gaze made him break off. He looked from her to the tree, across the street at the Somerville property, then back to the tree again. "Well, well," he said. "We were just going to see Somerville. There were some questions we wanted to ask him, but I think we could take a few minutes to help a chap get his kite, don't you, Sergeant?"

Tucker may have been large and slow-moving, but he was not slow-witted.

"I think so too. Come on, young 'un."

He walked over to the beech tree with Andrew, picked him up, and lifted him to the full stretch of his arms. This was high enough for Andrew to grasp the tree's lowest branches and, pulling himself up, he began climbing. Sara, Wyatt, and the sergeant moved back and, since the buds were only beginning to show and the tree had no leaves yet, they were able to follow his progress until he was more than halfway to the top.

"He's a good climber," said Tucker. "He's going up like a naval cadet."

"Yes," said Sara. "Any news?"

"About what?" asked Wyatt.

"The Somerville case. Or the Polk murder case, if that's what you're calling it."

"We're calling it the Somerville case, and . . . yes, there is some news. We found the carriage Polk rented."

"Where?"

"Hampstead."

"Were there any clues, anything that could tell you who had stolen it?"

"No. The horses had been driven hard—they were all lathered—but they hadn't been hurt and the brougham was undamaged. And of course the chest Somerville talked about and all the luggage was gone."

"Then you've still got no lead."

"Not really, no."

"Too bad." She stepped back, peering upward. "I've lost Andrew. Can you see him?"

"Yes," said Tucker. "He's almost at the top of the tree, but he's not climbing at the moment. He's looking off that way." And he pointed toward the Somerville house.

"I wonder why," said Sara.

"I can't imagine," said Wyatt.

"He's going on again," said Tucker. "There, he's got the kite."

Andrew had come around to their side of the tree now, and they watched as he pulled the kite free and tossed it wide so that it dangled from the lower branches of the tree by its string. Tucker pulled it down and began winding up the line. By the time he had finished, Andrew had reached the lowest large branch, hung from it for a moment, then dropped to the ground.

"There you are," said Tucker, giving him the kite. "A few holes in it that you can patch, but outside of that as good as new."

"Thank you," said Andrew. Then, conversationally, "You know, while I was up there, I found I could look over the wall of the Somerville property."

"Did you?" said Wyatt in the same offhanded manner.

"Yes. And it was quite interesting."

"In what way?"

"Well, the wall encloses a fairly good sized bit of land, large enough to make a very nice garden. But while there are a few trees and some grass and flower beds, the most important thing there, right in the center, is a small house."

"A summer house?"

"No. It's a very solid house, built of brick. It has a heavy wooden door and there are bars on the windows."

"Oh?" said Wyatt.

"Maybe that's where Lord Somerville used to keep his valuables," said Sara. "The things he was worried about. They'd be pretty safe there, especially if he had a watchdog wandering around loose at night."

"That's what I thought at first. And that may be the

reason for the house. But there was something else that was a little strange." Andrew pointed toward the wall. "You see those spikes on top of the wall that curve out so that no one can climb in from the outside?"

"Yes."

"Well, there's another set just like them on the inside that are curved *in*. And that made me wonder if Lord Somerville or whoever built the wall wasn't just as concerned about keeping someone or something *in* as keeping people out."

"I see," said Wyatt soberly. "Curiouser and curiouser as a certain young person remarked ungrammatically."

"Yes, it is," said Tucker. "Do you think Lord Somerville might explain it if we asked him about it?"

"No, I don't," said Wyatt. "As a matter of fact, I think we'll forget about talking to him right now. Because I've a feeling we might find out a good deal more from him if we knew a bit more."

"About what?" asked Sara.

"About several things. Thank you, Andrew. As usual, you've been both ingenious and helpful. Come on, Sergeant. Let's go back to the station house."

"Wait a minute," said Sara. "You mean you're not going to tell us . . . Inspector!"

If Wyatt heard her, he gave no sign of it, but walked back toward Wellington Road with Tucker.

"Well, I like that!" said Sara. "Do you know what he was talking about? What he wants to find out?"

"No," said Andrew. "At least . . . no."

He may not have known then, but an idea must have come to him soon afterward, for when Sara went looking for him later that afternoon, she found him in the library studying a thick book.

"What are you reading?" she asked.

"Bradshaw."

"What's Bradshaw?"

"The railway guide. It gives timetables for all the railways in England."

"Are you going somewhere?"

"I'm thinking about it."

"Where?"

"Ansley Cross."

Her eyes widened. "That's where Lord Somerville's country place is—where he lived before he came to London."

"That's right."

"Does this have anything to do with what Wyatt was interested in? What he wanted to find out about?"

"It's possible."

"Of course it is. When are we going?"

"We?"

"You go without me and see what happens!"

"I wouldn't dare," he said smiling. "I thought we might go tomorrow. There's a train out of Paddington at three minutes after nine."

"I'll tell Mum."

"What will you tell her?"

"That we're going down to the country for the day."

"Will that be all right with her?"

"If I'm going with you, it will."

"What have I done to deserve such trust?"

"I don't know, but it does come in handy at times."

As Sara had expected, Mrs. Wiggins raised no objection to the trip. They caught the 9:03 from Paddington, and all went well until the train stopped at Reading where they had to change. Andrew opened the door of the compartment, then paused.

"What is it?" asked Sara.

"Look up there, at the other end of the platform."

"Wyatt!" she said, peering out. "He must be going to Ansley Cross, too."

"Yes."

"Do you think he'll be angry if he sees us?"

"He might be."

"What'll we do?"

"Well, if he *is* angry, he might insist that we go home. Theres' a train back to London in about a half hour. But if he doesn't see us till we get to Ansley Cross, there won't be anything he can do about it because the only train from there back here is at three-thirty."

"Behind that baggage cart?"

"Yes." He peered out again, then, since Wyatt had his back turned, walking up the platform, he said, "Now!"

They jumped out of the compartment, ran around behind the baggage cart, which was piled high with crates and trunks, and waited there. When the branch line train came in, they waited to see which car Wyatt got in and got in the one behind it.

It took about twenty minutes to get to their station, and though they had started out feeling quite pleased with themselves, by the time the train stopped, they weren't so sure that what they'd done was a good idea. Wyatt got out, walked to the end of the platform and stood there looking up the road. They got out more tentatively, hesitated for a moment, uncertain as to how to approach him.

"Well, come on," he said, his back to them. "The trap'll be here any minute."

"How did you know we were here?" asked Sara.

"Next time you're trying to hide from someone, remember that it's very easy to see underneath a baggage cart. Your two pairs of legs, taken in conjunction, are quite unmistakeable."

"Oh," said Andrew. "Then you're not angry?"

"If I was, I've had twenty minutes to get over it. I take it that you didn't follow me—that you thought of coming down here by yourselves."

"Yes."

"Dr. Owen thought that I took you around with me to distract people, make them forget who I am and what

I'm after. But you know that's not true. You distract me more than you do anyone else."

"But you've got to admit that we've helped you," said Sara.

"Yes. That's why I'm not sending you packing." Then, as a trap appeared around a curve in the road and approached the station. "This should be our transportation."

The trap drew up at the station, and the driver—an alert, grey-haired man in uniform—said, "Inspector Wyatt?"

"Yes."

"I'm Constable Lowrie. Sorry if I kept you waiting, but we only got your telegram late this morning."

"It doesn't matter. These are colleagues of mine, unofficial plainclothes agents, Sara Wiggins and Andrew Tillett."

"Unofficial? They look quite official to me," said Lowrie gravely. "I think there's room for all of you." He waited till they had all climbed into the trap, Wyatt sitting beside him and Sara and Andrew behind them. Then, shaking the reins, he sent the horse trotting down the road. "You said in your wire that you were on a case that involved Lord Somerville."

"That's correct. He was robbed, and the caretaker of his London house was killed."

"I read about that. He wasn't hurt himself?"

"No. But although he told us a good deal about himself and his background, there were some things I thought I'd like to look into myself down here."

"Naturally, I'll be happy to do anything I can to help. Have you any idea of where you'd like to begin?"

"I think at the Somerville estate."

"Greyhurst? We may have a little trouble there. The house has been closed up for years, and I doubt if old Duncan, who looks after it, would let even you in without specific instructions from his lordship."

"I'm afraid it never occurred to me to discuss that with him. What about the grounds?"

"Duncan knows me, so I think we can manage that."

"Good. I take it you know Somerville."

"Yes, I do. Not well, of course, but better than most folks in these parts. My father was gamekeeper, first for his father and then for him."

"I see. Do you know why he closed Greyhurst and moved in to London?"

"I think I have some idea. It's a sad story. And what makes it worse is that we always thought of the Randalls as a lucky family."

"The Randalls?" said Sara.

"Randall is the family name," explained Wyatt. "Somerville is the title."

"It's Lord Somerville of Greyhurst," said Lowrie. "As I said, we always thought of them as lucky. The present Lord Somerville's father died peacefully at a good age, and he himself had a very good marriage. Then suddenly everything changed."

"How?"

"He married Lord Barham's daughter. After the marriage, he made only one trip to Mesopotamia or wherever he goes and her ladyship went with him. When they came back, it was clear that she was going to have a child."

"When was this?"

"Oh, fifteen, sixteen years ago, the year we had that terrible winter. In February, during the worst storm of the year, she had the child. By all reports, she had a very hard time of it. His Lordship had gone into London, couldn't get back, and Dr. Roberts, who had been taking care of her, had a great deal of trouble getting to Greyhurst. By the time he did, the child had been born, and shortly after that, right after Lord Somerville got home, her ladyship died."

"I see. That is sad. Was the child all right?"

"Why, yes. So far as I know. It was a boy, and they named him Alfred, his grandfather's name. Abby Severn took care of him."

"Is that Mrs. Severn?"

"Yes. She was a local girl, Abby Diggs she was till she got married. She'd come to Greyhurst early on to help out because she was having a child, too. But her child died, and so she stayed on and nursed the boy, Alfred."

"She must have done more than act as nurse," said Wyatt. "She's still with Somerville in London, acting as his housekeeper."

"I'm not surprised. His lordship thought a great deal of her, pretty well left her in charge when he went away. And he was away most of the time from then on."

"Where's the boy now?" asked Andrew. "Somerville's son?"

"At a school in Switzerland. At least, that's what I heard. And I believe that's why he closed Greyhurst. He got rid of most of the staff here after her ladyship died—I guess he couldn't bear to stay here—or even in England, for that matter. And then, about five years ago, when the boy went to Switzerland, he took a place in London."

"And now he's about to move to Paris," said Wyatt.

"Well, he would be closer to Switzerland there than in London," said Andrew.

"That's true," said Wyatt. "And he also claimed he had been doing a good deal of work with a French Assyriologist. But . . ."

They had been driving along a lane since shortly after they left the station, a narrow lane lined with hedges that were just beginning to bud. Now they came out of the lane, and there was a wall to their right, meadows to their left. Sara had been strangely silent during the drive and, looking at her, Andrew realized that though she may have been listening to everything that was said—city girl that she was—she had also been fascinated by her surroundings; the hedges alive with nesting birds and now the green fields with the cattle in them. Then, as a lark flew up and burst into song, "Coo!" she said. "What's that?"

"Skylark," said Andrew. "Isn't it?"

"Yes," said Lowrie. "Some think they've got the prettiest song of any bird. Myself, I've always been partial to blackbirds."

He drew up in front of a pair of closed iron gates. There was a stone lodge just inside them.

"If you don't mind waiting a minute, I'll go have a word with old Duncan."

He handed Wyatt the reins, got down from the trap and went over to the gate. A white-haired man with chin whiskers came out of the lodge and nodded to Lowrie.

"What's that?" asked Sara, pointing to a shield-shaped carving cut into the wall to the right of the gate.

"The Somerville coat of arms," said Wyatt. "Azure, three acorns gold and two rondels in the chief."

"But azure's blue, isn't it?"

"Yes. A coat of arms is meant to be painted on a shield. If it *were* painted, the background would be blue and the three acorns below and the two circles above would be gold."

"You do know a lot, don't you?"

"Not really. I've just been doing a little research on

the Randalls. They're an old and quite famous family."

The white-haired man had been looking at them through the fretted ironwork of the gates. Finally he nodded, took a large key out of his pocket, unlocked the gates and pulled them open.

"I was right," said Lowrie, climbing back into the trap. "He says he can't let us into the house without instructions from his lordship, but that it's all right if we drive around the grounds. Will that be of any help?"

"It's better than nothing," said Wyatt. "If I feel it's necessary, I'll come back with a letter from Somerville."

Lowrie shook the reins and sent the horse trotting past the gate house and up the drive, which was lined with huge trees—elms and oaks and beeches. Though there was no longer any resident staff, arrangements must have been made for workmen to come in and tend the grounds, for the underbrush had been cut and in general what they could see looked cared for. This was not true of the house when they finally reached it. It was a huge building, built of grey stone with deep-set windows and a heavy wooden door studded and rein-forced with iron bands. Its shutters were closed, and the ivy that covered most of the walls was beginning to spread over the windows. The grounds that they had come through had not only been cared for but were very much alive; rabbits had run across the drive in front of them, squirrels chattered in the trees and birds flew overhead. But there was no sound or sense of life in the house. Still and brooding, it was like a place under a spell.

"I'm glad we can't get in," said Sara. "It would scare the wits out of me."

"I'm not sure I'd like it much myself," said Lowrie.

Wyatt got out of the trap and walked away from the building, looking up at the facade from the far side of the driveway.

"Do you know the place well?" he asked Lowrie.

"Well, no. I've only been in it a few times, and I've never been all through it. Why?"

"What are those rooms up there?" he asked, pointing to some windows at the left-hand side of an upper story.

"Let's see," said Lowrie. "The kitchen's on that side, in the back. The next floor's bedrooms. I think those were Master Alfred's quarters, the nursery and school room."

"Then why are there bars on the windows?"

"Bars? Where?" Lowrie joined Wyatt on the far side of the driveway. "Strange. I never noticed them before. They were probably put there to keep the children from falling out. After all, the windows are up pretty high."

"Yes, they are," said Wyatt. He looked at the building again, then said, "I think I've seen enough for the time being. If there's anything else I want to look at, I'll come back."

"Righto," said Lowrie.

They got back into the trap, Lowrie shook the reins and the horse trotted on along the driveway, circling around and going out toward the gate.

"You said Mrs. Severn was a local woman," said Wyatt. "Was her husband local, too?"

"Sixty? Yes, he was."

"Was that his name, Sixty? I thought it was Tom."

"His proper name was Tom, but he was known as Sixty—don't ask me why, because I don't know."

"What kind of person was he?"

"What kind? The kind we can do without!"

"You knew him well?"

"The only ones who knew him better were our magistrates and the wardens at various clinks. My father had him up for poaching when he was sixteen. He was sent away twice after that, and of course he ended up at Dartmoor after he'd been found guilty of robbery and assault."

"Yes, I know about that. But then why did Abby Diggs marry him?"

"Well, he was a good looking man in his own gypsy way and, in the beginning, she must have thought he was just wild, not bad. Like most women, she must have thought she could get him to change, reform. By the time she found out the truth, she *had* to marry him. Not that he ever saw his child. It was born after Sixty was sent away."

"What happened to the child?"

"He died just before the Somerville child was born. That was one of the reasons Abby was able to nurse young Alfred. Not that she wouldn't have been able to nurse both of them if her own child had lived. A strong young woman she was."

"And still is."

"Has any of this been of any help to you?"

"I'm not sure, but I think perhaps it has. There's one more thing I'd like to do while I'm down here and that's talk to the doctor who attended Lady Somerville. You said his name was Roberts?"

"Yes. But I'm afraid you won't be able to. He's not here anymore."

"Oh? Where is he?"

"I don't know. I said it was a sad story as far as the Randalls were concerned. But I'm afraid it was sad for the doctor, too. Not that he hadn't been having a certain amount of trouble anyway. His wife ran off and left him —they say she found the life out here too lonely—and that was a bad blow to him. He was a bit queer after that, and people thought maybe he was taking laudanum—not that there was ever a sign of it in his work: he was still a very good doctor, the best around here. But right after the Randall baby was born, he had a bad accident—as I said, it was one of the worst winters anyone remembers, lots of snow and ice. His carriage turned over and hurt his legs so that he could hardly walk after that. That made it difficult for him to carry on a country practice, so he sold out and left."

"And went where?"

"I'm not really sure—either Canada or South Africa. Out of the country anyway."

"I see. Too bad. Then I guess that's that. The next item on the agenda is lunch. Is there any place near here that you'd recommend?"

"Well, The Barley Mow near the station does one pretty well."

"Good. You'll join us of course."

"That's kind of you, Inspector. Thank you."

Lowrie drove them to the inn, which was just a short distance from the station, and had lunch with them. It was a very good lunch; veal and ham pies all around, with ale for Wyatt and Lowrie and ginger beer for Sara and Andrew. Wyatt kept Lowrie talking all through lunch—about the Randalls and the area around Ansley Cross in general—and Sara and Andrew kept discreetly silent. It was only after Lowrie had driven them to the station, had been thanked and left, that Wyatt turned to them and said, "Well, chums, any thoughts?"

"A few," said Sara.

"For instance?"

"Those bars on the windows of young Alfred's rooms. When you want to make sure that a child won't fall out, don't you run the bars across—and then only part way up—instead of all the way up and down?"

"Usually. There's a curious parallel between those windows and the ones Andrew reported seeing in the small house inside the grounds on Alder Road."

"That's what I thought," said Andrew. "Does all that make things any clearer to you?"

"Let's say it's given me a good deal more to think about—which is sometimes a help. I think I should have another talk with Mrs. Severn. And perhaps with the injured Sixty, too."

"It just occurred to me that someone else it might be interesting to talk to is Pierre."

"Who's Pierre?"

Andrew told him. Wyatt vaguely remembered seeing a chimney sweep and his boy when they left the pub after their meeting with Polk, but he had not seen them join Severn. He was quite interested in that, and even more interested in what had happened the next morning, the fact that the chimney sweep had been in the crowd when Polk had talked to the constable about the dog that had been killed.

"How do you know that the boy's name is Pierre?" he asked.

Sara told that part of it; of how the butcher's boy and the others had been baiting Pierre and Andrew had intervened, talked to him and learned that he was French.

"What's he doing here?" asked Wyatt. "How did he get here?"

"We don't know," said Andrew. "The sweep came

along and took him away before he could tell us."

"I see. Yes, it would be interesting to talk to him. I don't suppose you know where we can get hold of him."

"No. He knows where we live, but . . ."

"How does he know that?"

Sara told him about the stable boy who had recognized them, mentioned where they lived, and how Pierre had repeated it as he was leaving.

"Well, it's not likely that he'll come looking for you," said Wyatt. "But after what you've told me about him, it might be worth while trying to find him."

6

Looking for Pierre

"I've been thinking," said Sara.

"About what?"

"About Pierre. Why was the inspector so anxious to find him?"

"Because, if that scarecrow of a chimney sweep he works for is a friend of Severn's, Pierre just might know something that could be useful."

"That's what I thought," said Sara. "And I've an idea about how I might find him. Pierre, I mean."

Andrew looked at her. It was early afternoon on the day after their trip down to Ansley Cross, and they were out on the lawn in back of the house playing badminton.

"Just you?" he said.

"Yes."

"How?"

"I'd rather not say."

"Why not?"

"Because you'll try and talk me out of it."

"I'd only do that if what you were going to do was dangerous."

"It's not. But you might not like it for other reasons."

"What other reasons?"

"I'm not going to say because then you'd probably guess, and I don't care if you like it or not because I think I should do it and, with Mum and Fred both going to be away, this is the perfect time for it."

"Well, I don't know if that's what you intended, but you've certainly got me intrigued."

"That's good. Then you won't try to stop me?"

"Could I?"

"Well, you could kind of spoil things by insisting on coming along."

"You mean it's something you've got to do alone?"

"Yes. But I'll make a deal with you. You can come along if you keep far enough away so that no one'll know you're with me."

Andrew hesitated, bouncing the shuttlecock on his racket.

"All right. Sold to the lady in blue. When do we start?"

"As soon as Mum and Fred go. In the meantime, let's play. What's the score?"

"Eleven to nine. I'm serving."

He stepped back, batted the shuttlecock over the high

net, and she hit it back, placing it so that he had to race to get it. She may not have played cricket or rugger—no girls did—but anything she did play, like badminton, she played hard and well. He had lost the serve, and they were ten to eleven when Fred drove the landau out of the stable and around to the front of the house.

They followed and were standing there when Mrs. Wiggins came out. She was going to Peter Robinson's on Oxford Street to buy linens for the house. They were badly needed but, even though Andrew's mother had been urging her to get them for some time, she had insisted on waiting until they were on sale. This of course was one of the reasons she was such a splendid housekeeper, something everyone knew she was except Mrs. Wiggins herself.

"How do I look?" she asked.

She was wearing her best dress and a hat and coat that Andrew's mother had given her and looked, not just respectable, but quite distinguished.

"You look fine, Mum."

"Are you sure?"

"I'm sure."

"You do, Mrs. Wiggins," said Andrew. "You look really handsome."

"I don't want to look handsome. I just want to look all right. But if you think I do . . ." She got into the landau; Fred closed the door and climbed up to the box. "I'll see you at about tea time."

"Yes, mum. Goodbye."

They watched the carriage go down the driveway and turn right toward Wellington Road.

"Now what?" asked Andrew.

"I have to get some things from the house. Wait for me in the stable."

Andrew stopped in the kitchen, got some carrots and was feeding them to the grey hunter that shared the stable with the carriage horses when Sara entered.

"What have you got there?" Andrew asked, looking at the bundle she was carrying.

"Clothes. I didn't want to change in the house because I didn't want anyone asking me questions. But if you'll wait out in the mews, I'll be with you in a couple of minutes."

"Right."

"And remember, you can follow me if you like, but don't talk to me or do anything that will let anyone know you know me."

"Right," he said again and went through the stable and out the back way that led to the mews. He walked up the alley toward Alder Road and paused at the entrance to the last stable, the one that belonged to the Marchioness of Medford. Her coachman was sitting just inside the door mending a harness strap. He was a friend of Fred's and a cricket buff, and he and Andrew immediately got into an argument about England's chances against the visiting Australian team. Andrew was baiting him into offering fairly long odds on the Australians, and had gotten him to three-to-one, when someone walked by behind him. He looked over his shoulder, saw that it was a dirty-faced ragamuffin of a girl and was going on with his discussion when something about her caught his attention, he looked again and saw that it was Sara.

Closing the bet with the coachman, Andrew excused himself and went after her. She turned left on Alder Road, walking toward the Somerville house, and he followed some distance behind her. Even studying her closely, he found it difficult to tell what she had done to make herself look so different. Granted that her dress was old and torn, in much worse condition than the one she had worn when he had first met her. And granted that the shoes she was wearing were not her own—they were much too large—and that her face was dirty and her hair unkempt, there was still something else. And it was only when she rang the bell of the service door at the Somerville house that he realized what it was. It was the way she walked and carried herself; half awkward and defensive, and half impudent and ready to battle against any slight or slur. Like a first-rate actress, she had completely *become* the character she was playing; in this case, a slovenly street urchin.

The service door opened, and a severe looking woman in a dark dress, whom Andrew assumed was Mrs. Severn, looked out. Bobbing in an awkward curtsey, Sara began talking to her and, though Andrew was too far away to hear what she said, he knew that that would be in character, too; that it would be in as broad a Cockney as she had originally spoken, before Andrew's mother had begun teaching her proper speech.

Mrs. Severn said something to Sara then, apparently in response to a question of some sort, shook her head and went back into the house. Andrew remained where he was, behind the beech tree across the street from the Somerville house, and watched as Sara went to the next house, rang the bell at the service door there, and engaged in a colloquy with a rather dumpy woman who may have been another housekeeper but could also have been a cook. In all, Sara stopped off at nine houses, four on each side of the Somerville house; then, looking over her shoulder, she jerked her head at Andrew and walked west toward Wellington Road.

"Well?" he said, catching up with her, "Did you get your ear full?"

He said this in his own best Cockney, and she gave him a half appreciative and half rueful smile.

"No. At least, it didn't turn out the way I hoped."

"Well, tell anyway."

"First, there's who I was—and that's a poor girl whose father's a chimney sweep."

"The tall scarecrow of a sweep that Pierre works for?"

"Yes."

"What were you doing here?"

"Looking for dad. Because he was a dabeno, a real bad one, who left mom and me a few months ago. But we heard he'd been seen around here and wanted to find him."

"How could anyone around here help you?"

"How do you think sweeps get work? Besides shouting 'Sweep!' they knock at doors, and if people don't want the sweeping done right then, they leave a card or say, 'A word at the coal dealer's will always find me.'"

"And you thought if that particular sweep had done that, it would lead us to Pierre."

"That's right. But you know what? The boyo we're looking for stopped off at only one house around here. Do you know which one?"

"Lord Somerville's."

"Right. Mrs. Severn—at least I think it was Mrs. Severn—said he knocked at the door sometime last week, asked if she wanted sweeping done and offered to do it real cheap."

"Are you sure it was the chap we want?"

"Certain sure. I started to describe him, and she did it for me—tall and thin as a beanpole. She even remembered Pierre—a very little, white-faced boy with very big eyes."

"And did he sweep for her?"

"No. She said she didn't need it done, didn't let him in."

"I see. Now what do you think he was after?"

"I think I know."

"Of course you do. I think this is something we should tell Wyatt."

"So do I."

They went up the street, turned right on Wellington Road, and went into the police station. Wyatt had told Andrew that when he was on a case he generally spent more time at the local station house, working with the detective who was based there and knew the area—in this case, Tucker—than he did at Scotland Yard. However they had forgotten how Sara looked until the desk sergeant frowned at them.

"Yes?" he said.

"We'd like to talk to Inspector Wyatt," said Andrew. "Is he here?"

"Maybe he is and maybe he isn't. What do you want with him?"

"We told you what we want," said Sara. "We want to talk to him. So don't give us any of your lip but just tell him we're here."

"Yes, m'lady," said the sergeant ironically. "And what names shall I give him?"

"Sara Wiggins and Andrew Tillett."

There's no telling with what witticism the sergeant would have responded to this if, at that moment a door to the left of the desk had not opened and Tucker looked out.

"Oh, it's you," he said with no particular surprise. "Were you looking for the inspector?"

"Yes."

"Come on in then."

They went in. The room was only slightly larger than Wyatt's office at Scotland Yard. The desk was, if anything, older and more battered. Wyatt, sitting at it and going over some notes, looked up at them, particularly at Sara.

"What are you dressed up for?" he asked.

"You said we were unofficial plainclothes agents. We've been doing some investigating. At least, I have."

"Have you?"

"Yes. You said you'd like to talk to Pierre, so we thought we'd try to find him for you. We didn't, but we found out something else."

"What was that?"

"The flue faker he works for—the tall, thin one—was at the Somerville house last week, wanted to clean the chimneys there, but Mrs. Severn wouldn't let him in. And that was the *only* house he went to—he didn't go to any others around here."

"Fascinating," said Wyatt dryly.

"You don't sound fascinated."

"I was mildly interested when I first found it out."

"You already knew it?"

"Yes."

"How did you find out about it?"

"The way the C.I.D. usually finds things out. I asked Sergeant Tucker to go around this morning and inquire."

"Oh," said Sara.

"What do you think it means?" asked Andrew.

"What do *you* think it means?"

"Well, we know—or at least we're pretty sure—that there's some connection between Severn and the tall, thin sweep."

"His name is Gann. Matty Gann."

"How do you know?"

"We looked him up. He has a record—not as serious as Severn's—but a record just the same."

"I see. You told us Severn had gone to the house but Mrs. Severn wouldn't let him in or even talk to him. Well, if I were Severn and I was anxious to find out what was going on there, I might get a pal who was a chimney sweep to stop by, because a sweep goes all through a house and can see almost anything he wants."

Tucker and Wyatt exchanged glances.

"Not bad," said Tucker.

"Is that what you thought, too?" asked Sara.

"Yes," said Wyatt. "Now listen to me and listen very carefully. You're both very bright and you've been almost as helpful on this case as you were on the Denham diamond case, but you've done enough. This is not a game. It's a serious and dangerous case. There's been one murder already—Sergeant Polk—and I wouldn't be surprised if there were more deaths. So I want you to mind your own business and stay out of things from now on. If you should run across the boy, Pierre, or discover where I can reach him, fine. Let me know. But, apart from that, you're to avoid any connection with the case. Is that clear?"

Solemnly, they nodded.

"All right. Run along then and let us get on with what we're doing."

7

The Second Murder

Wyatt had meant to be emphatic, not prophetic; but, as often happens when there is validity to someone's concern, what he warned them about came to pass. Before it did, however—or at least before Sara and Andrew learned about it—something else of equal importance happened.

It happened that night and, because Andrew's room was in the front of the house, he was the first to be aware of it. They went home after their talk with Wyatt at the police station, hurrying a bit because Sara wanted to wash up and change her clothes before her mother came home. After supper they played parcheesi and, as she sometimes did, Mrs. Wiggins joined them, though she had some reservations about any game that involved dice.

They went up to bed at about ten o'clock, and Andrew read for a while. He was reading Stevenson's *The Strange Case of Dr. Jekyll and Mr. Hyde,* which he found disturbing as well as fascinating, and that may have been why he did not sleep particularly well. He woke up sometime later with a feeling that someone had been calling him. He lay there for a moment, listening. The house was quiet, and there was no sound but the solemn ticking of the grandfather clock out on the landing. Nevertheless the feeling that someone had called him was so strong that he got out of bed, went to the door and opened it. Still nothing. While he was there, he looked at the clock. It was ten after two. He went back into his room but, before he got back into bed, he looked out of the window. The moon was almost full and, though a few clouds were passing overhead, for the most part the front lawn was brightly lit. And, lying on the grass near the driveway, face down and arms out-stretched, was a small figure. Though he couldn't be sure, Andrew thought he knew who it was.

Stepping into his slippers, he put on his robe, hurried to the door and opened it again. This time the door of Sara's room opened, and she came out.

"I thought I heard you," she whispered. "What is it?"

"Someone outside, lying on the lawn. It looks as if he's been hurt."

"Who is it?"

"I'm not sure, but I think it's Pierre."

"Oh!" Her eyes widened. "Shall I wake Mum?"

"Perhaps you'd better. I'll go down in the meantime and see."

Sara ran up the corridor toward her mother's room, and Andrew went downstairs. The door was not only locked and bolted, it had a chain on it too, and it took him several minutes to get it open. He ran down the driveway and discovered he had been right. The figure on the lawn was Pierre. Except for his outstretched arms, he was crumpled up and very still. Turning him over gently, Andrew saw that his eyes were closed and there was blood on his face. He knelt down, pressed his ear to the French boy's chest, listening for his heart beat. When he finally heard it, it seemed very faint. As he straightened up, Sara and Mrs. Wiggins came out, both wearing robes over their nightclothes.

"*Is* it Pierre?" asked Sara.

"Yes."

"What's wrong with him?"

"I'm not sure. There's a nasty gash on his head—I think he was hit there. But besides that, he's soaking wet, as if he's been in water somewhere."

"He looks bad, the poor child," said Mrs. Wiggins. Then, as Matson, the butler, came out carrying a lit candle, "Do you think you and Matson can carry him upstairs to the guest room?"

"Of course. I could probably do it alone."

"You'd better do it together, then you won't shake him up so much. Meanwhile, Sara, you go wake Fred and tell him to go get Dr. Davison."

The doctor, whose surgery was on Wimpole Street, lived nearby on Alder Road. He had been to the house a few times on calls and was a great admirer of Andrew's mother.

"Yes, Mum," said Sara and went running off, her hair flying.

Though Matson was usually very distant and reserved, Andrew found him strangely human in this particular emergency. Even Pierre's torn and ragged clothes did not seem to upset him unduly, and together they un-dressed the unconscious boy and put a pajama top of Andrew's on him—it was much too big of course—before they tucked him into the guest room bed.

"Do you see any reason for keeping these, Master Andrew?" asked Matson, picking up the torn and damp clothes they had dropped on the floor.

"No, Matson, I don't."

"I shall dispose of them, then." And, holding them at arm's length, he went out and down the back stairs.

Mrs Wiggins came in, and when Sara came back from calling Fred, there was a brief discussion as to whether they should do anything while waiting for Dr. Davison; sponge off the wound on Pierre's head, try to give him some hot soup or brandy. They decided that since the doctor would be there very soon, it might be best to wait.

Dr. Davison arrived about fifteen minutes later, carrying his black bag. He greeted Andrew, nodded to Mrs. Wiggins and Sara and asked them to wait outside, but let Andrew stay while he examined Pierre.

"How did the boy come here?" he asked, putting his stethoscope back in his bag. "Do you know him?"

"I certainly don't know him well," said Andrew. "I only talked to him once. But I don't think he knows anyone else in London—at least, no one he considers a friend. He's French, and he's only been here a short time."

"I see. Besides this wound on his head—and besides the fact that he seems to have been beaten and starved—I find curious burns and lesions on his hands, elbows and knees. Can you explain them?"

"I think so. He works for a chimney sweep."

"Yes," said the doctor. "That would account for them. By law, chimney sweeps are not supposed to use climbing boys. At least, they're not supposed to send them up into the flues. But of course they do. I think I'll have a word with the police about it." He opened the door. "You can come in now," he said to Sara and Mrs. Wiggins.

"How is he? asked Sara.

"I think he'll be all right."

"You mean you're not sure about it?" asked Andrew.

"Well, he isn't in very good shape. Besides malnutrition, he has a concussion—that's why he's unconscious—and it's hard to say how long he'll remain that way. The question is, can you take care of him here or should I put him in St. George's?"

"You mean in hospital?"

"Yes."

Andrew and Sara exchanged quick looks with Mrs. Wiggins.

"We'll take care of him here," she said.

"You're sure you can manage?"

"If you'll tell us what to do, quite sure."

"Good. At the moment, just keep him warm and quiet. I'll stop by again in the morning with some medication for him, and we'll go over everything else."

"Yes, Doctor."

"There's one more thing," said Andrew. "Inspector Wyatt should be told."

"Yes, he should," said Sara.

Andrew glanced out into the hall where Fred was waiting.

"If you'll just give me a minute to put on some clothes, Doctor, I'll come along with you."

"Of course."

"You want to go to the police station now?" said Fred after they had dropped the doctor at his house.

"Do you know what time it is?"

"About three-thirty."

"Well, who do you expect to find there?"

"The desk sergeant. If I leave a message with him, the inspector will have it when he comes in tomorrow morning."

"All right, me boyo. But a quid to a Brummagem sixpence, the sergeant won't like it. Because he'll be sleeping as sound as I wish I was."

Andrew should have taken Fred's bet because, when they got to the police station, there were more signs of activity there than there usually were during the day. A growler was standing in front of the door, the cabby walking up and down as he waited. There was a light on in the small office Wyatt used, and, when Andrew went into the station, there were two constables at the desk as well as the sergeant behind it. They all looked at Andrew but, before he could tell them what he wanted, the door of Wyatt's office opened and Tucker came out.

"Oh, no," he said. "Not you again. What did the inspector tell you?"

"It's because of what he said that I'm here."

Tucker looked at him sharply. "Half a sec." He went back to the office door, said something and, a moment later, Wyatt appeared. He was frowning and clearly had something on his mind, for he said nothing about the lateness of the hour, but only, "What is it, Andrew?"

"You wanted us to let you know if we found Pierre or discovered where to reach him. Well, we have. He's at the house."

"At your house?"

"Yes. We've got him in bed."

"Why in bed?"

"He showed up about an hour ago. He had been hit on the head and is unconscious now. The doctor says he's not sure how long he'll stay that way. But I thought you'd want to know anyway."

"Yes. Thanks for letting me know. I'll stop by and see how he is tomorrow." He turned to the two constables. "All right, men."

Tucker opened the station house door, and the two constables went out.

"Has anything happened?" asked Andrew as Wyatt buttoned up his coat and prepared to follow them.

"Yes. I think you can say something else has happened. There's been another murder."

Andrew stared at him for a moment. That was why Wyatt had shown so little interest in the news about Pierre.

"In the Somerville case?"

"Yes. In the Somerville case."

8

The False Clue

Lord Somerville was at breakfast the next morning when the front doorbell jangled. Pushing aside the toast that he had barely touched, he looked up when the dining room door opened and Mrs. Severn came in.

"It's Inspector Wyatt and Sergeant Tucker," she said. "They'd like a word with you."

"Oh?" He tried to read her expression but couldn't. "Well, send them in."

"Yes, m'lord."

Somerville finished his tea and stood up as Wyatt and Tucker entered.

"Good morning, Inspector. Good morning, Sergeant. You're up and about early."

"Not too early for you, I hope," said Wyatt.

"No, no. I've finished my breakfast. Can I offer you anything?"

"Thank you, no. We had our breakfast some hours ago."

"Hours?"

"Yes."

"Well, sit down then. Mrs. Severn said you wanted to talk to me."

"Yes, we do," said Wyatt. He sat down at the table facing Somerville. Tucker crossed the room and sat in a chair against the wall where he could watch Somerville from the side.

"Does it have anything to do with what you were last here about?" asked Somerville. "Sergeant Polk's murder or the things that were stolen?"

"Yes," said Wyatt. "We think so."

"There's been some new development?"

"Yes."

"Will you tell me what it is?"

"Yes. But before I do, may I ask you a few questions?"

"Of course."

"Will you tell us where you were last night?"

"Last night?"

"Yes. Let's say from about nine o'clock on."

Somerville looked at him, at Tucker who sat with a pencil in his hand and his notebook open, then back to Wyatt again.

"Why, I was here."

"Here in the house?"

"Yes."

"You never went out at all?"

"No. Why?"

"Because there was another murder last night, probably around midnight."

Somerville's face, pale before, became ashen.

"Another murder?' 'he whispered.

"Yes. Polk's death was murder. This was a second murder."

"Who . . . who was it? I mean . . ."

"A woman. Not a young woman and probably not a very nice one. But still murder is murder."

"Yes, of course. But why did you ask me where I was?"

"Because of this." Wyatt took something out of his pocket, put it on the table in front of Somerville. "Does it mean anything to you?"

Somerville picked it up and looked at it. His face could not have become paler or more bloodless, but he suddenly seemed to age, to look as he might in twenty years. For what he was holding was a shield-shaped gold cuff link with three acorns and two circles on it.

"It's my coat of arms," he said. "Where did you get it?"

"The woman's body was found in an alley off Pentonville Road. The cuff link was in her hand."

"I see," said Somerville. Wyatt had carefully avoided looking at the man's wrists, but now Somerville held them out. He was wearing a pair of cuff links that were similar to the one Wyatt had given him, except that they were older and more worn.

"Yes," said Wyatt. "But, as you can see, this one carries your coat of arms also. Can you tell me anything about it?"

"The ones I am wearing were my father's," said Somerville. "When I became twenty-one, he had another pair made and gave them to me. When he died, I put away the pair that he had given me and began wearing his links."

"Where did you put this other pair?"

"In a collar box with a few other personal things. The collar box was in the coach when it was stolen the night Polk was killed."

"I see," said Wyatt.

"Of course you only have my word for that as you have for my statement that I was here last night. But . . . Mrs. Severn," he called. He waited a moment, then called again, "Mrs. Severn."

The door opened and she came in.

"Yes, m'lord?"

"Where was I last night?"

"Here, m'lord."

"Here in the house?"

"Yes, m'lord."

"Did I leave it at any time?"

"No, m'lord. Not to my knowledge."

Wyatt nodded. "May I have that cuff link?" he said.

"It's evidence. Thank you." He put it in his pocket and rose. "Good day. And a good day to you too, Mrs. Severn."

Tucker had risen, too. They both bowed to Somerville and Mrs. Severn and went out.

"Well, Sergeant?" said Wyatt as they walked up the street. "What do you think?"

"He was very upset, there's no doubt about that. He was upset when we got there, and even more so when you told him about the murder. But I don't think he was lying. I don't think he did it On the other hand, how do you explain the cuff link?"

"There's no great problem about that." He stopped and faced Tucker. "I'm going to attack you with a knife. Grab my wrist to stop me." Tucker seized his wrist. "Now, as I pull away, what happens?"

"I'm holding your shirt sleeve, your cuff link."

"How are you holding it?"

"With my thumb and forefinger."

"And how was the dead woman holding it?"

"She wasn't holding it. It was in the palm of her hand."

"Where in her palm?"

"On the other side, near her little finger. But that might have happened—it might have moved there—when she fell."

"If she hadn't been holding it firmly, would it have remained in her hand at all? I doubt it. And if we had found it on the ground nearby, we might not have been suspicious. But finding it where we did, *did* make me suspicious. But of something else."

"You think someone put it in her hand, planted it there deliberately."

"Yes, I do."

Standing at the window, Mrs. Severn watched until Wyatt and Tucker were well up the street. Then she turned.

"They've gone," she said.

Somerville raised his head and looked at her bleakly.

"Did you hear?" he asked.

"Yes. What are you going to do?"

"There's nothing I can do. Or rather, only one thing."

9

The Encounter on the Bridge

Inspector Wyatt glanced at his watch as the church clock struck. Five o'clock. It seemed later than that, possibly because it was darker than it usually was at that hour. Getting up from his desk, he went to the window, looked out and saw why. A fog was settling down on the city. At the moment it was not too bad—he could still see the shops on the other side of Wellington Road—but, if he read the signs correctly, in an hour or so it would be really thick, a London particular.

A hansom drew up in front of the police station and Sergeant Tucker got out. He said something to the cabby who nodded, climbed down from his box in the rear, and began to walk up and down, clearly prepared to wait.

A moment later there was a knock on the office door.
"Come in, Sergeant," said Wyatt.

"Good afternoon, sir."

"Have you had tea?"

"No, sir."

"Neither have I. Why don't you give me your report, and we'll have the desk sergeant send some in for both of us?"

"Very good, sir." Taking out his notebook, he opened it and began to read, "Report on movements of occupants of sixty-two Alder Road."

"Never mind that. Just give me the highlights verbally."

"Right, sir. Mrs. Severn went out around nine-thirty, did some marketing and was back by ten-thirty. Lord Somerville went out a little after twelve, went to his club."

"The Travellers?"

"Yes. He was carrying a rather worn bag, a Gladstone, and at first I thought he might be leaving town and possibly the country, but he didn't. At about two o'clock he went to Lombard Street."

"To his bankers."

"Yes, sir. He was there until after three, and when he came out, he was still carrying the bag."

"Now what do you think he had in the bag, Sergeant?"

"I don't think it was Caerphilly cheese, sir."

"Nor do I. Then what?"

"He went home, back to Alder Road; and when I left, he was still there."

"Anything else?"

"Yes, something rather interesting. Just before I left, someone closed one of the parlor shutters and left the other one open. At the same time, a lit lamp was placed on the table near the window."

"A signal that he had the money."

"That would be my guess."

"You've got a good man covering the place now?"

"Yes. Wilkins."

"Good. Let's have our tea and we'll go over our plans for the next step."

Alone in his study, Lord Somerville was reading Bourdonne's monograph on cuneiform inscriptions when he heard someone walking rather quickly down Alder Road. Because of the fog, there had been few pedestrians abroad since he had had his solitary supper; but each time he heard footsteps, he waited tensely and, in every case so far, the walker had gone by without stopping. This time, however, the footsteps paused briefly, there was a light tap on the front door, then the footsteps went on again, more hurriedly than before. Putting down the monograph, Somerville took out his watch. It was five minutes after ten. He got up and was just starting for the door when it opened and Mrs. Severn came in.

He looked at her inquiringly, and she nodded and handed him a grimy, unstamped envelope, remained there, watching him while he opened it, took out a note and read it.

"Is it . . . ?" she asked.

"Yes. There are full instructions. I'll leave at midnight."

At about the same time, Andrew was opening the door of the guest room in the house on Rysdale Road. Mrs. Wiggins and Sara were both there; Mrs. Wiggins in an armchair near the head of the bed, Sara in a straight chair near its foot. Mrs. Wiggins's eyes were closed, her head had fallen forward, and she was snoring faintly. Andrew glanced at her, then at Sara. Wide awake, she smiled at him, and when he looked at Pierre and raised his eyebrows, she shook her head, indicating that he had not moved or regained consciousness since the doctor had left at about five o'clock.

Mrs. Wiggins sat up with a start and opened her eyes. "Oh!" she said. "What time is it?"

"A quarter after ten," said Andrew. "The two of you go to bed, and I'll take over."

"Do you really think that's necessary?"

"I do. We agreed that if he should come to and find himself alone in a strange place, it would be a great shock to him. So run along."

"You'll call me at midnight?" said Sara.

"Midnight or a little later, whenever I feel sleepy."

"And I'll take over again after Sara," said Mrs. Wiggins. She got up, stood there for a moment looking down at Pierre. "Poor lamb. I'm worried about him."

"The doctor said there was no reason to be. Not yet."

"I know. But still . . . would you like us to bring you something—some milk or biscuits?"

"No. I'm fine."

"I'll see you later, then," said Sara.

She and her mother left, and Andrew sat down in the straight chair where he could watch Pierre. He looked better than he had when they first found him. His face had been washed, his head bandaged and besides the medicine the doctor had given him, they had been able to get him to swallow some hot soup. But he still had not opened his eyes, had shown no signs of regaining consciousness. Suppose he never did? The doctor had assured them that that was very unlikely but, in the meantime, every hour that he remained unconscious was an hour lost; for Andrew and Sara were convinced—and Wyatt agreed—that he could tell them things that would help immeasurably in solving the several mysteries in the Somerville case.

At exactly midnight Lord Somerville left the house carrying the old Gladstone bag. Her face expressionless but strained, Mrs. Severn let him out, watched him start walking toward Wellington Road, then closed and locked the door.

Because of the hour and because of the fog, Somerville was not sure how long it would take him to find a cab. Left to his own devices, he would have started considerably earlier, but the instructions in the note had been very precise; he was to start out at midnight and not before. As it turned out, he was in luck. Before he reached Wellington Road, he heard the slow plod of hoofs and a hansom loomed up out of the murky darkness.

"Cab!" he called, stepping out into the street.

The hansom drew up. Though its side lights were lit, it was hard to see the driver who sat well above them. What Somerville did see, however, was not particularly reassuring, for the cabbie seemed to be a bleary-eyed, elderly man who sat huddled in the high seat with his hat tipped forward and a scarf wrapped around the lower part of his face. The reason for the scarf was quickly apparent for, as soon as he stopped the cab, he began coughing—a deep, racking asthmatic cough.

"I've a long way to go," said Somerville dubiously. "Are you up to it?"

"Not to worry, guv'ner," wheezed the cabby. "This cough's nothing. And I just come on duty so the old nag is fresh as a daisy."

The horse did look in better shape than most cab horses, so Somerville climbed into the hansom.

"Very well. Blackfriars Bridge."

"Righto, guv'ner."

Closing the door, the cabby turned the hansom, went back to Wellington Road and began the trip to Blackfriars. It was a long trip under any circumstances, and it took longer than usual on this particular night because of the fog, which meant that it was only at rare intervals that they could proceed faster than a walk. They went down Wellington Road, past the lower part of Regent's Park, down Baker Street, east on Oxford Street and Holborn, then south to the river on Farrington and New Bridge Streets. Between the fog and the lateness of the hour, they didn't pass more than three or four cabs on their whole journey nor more than half a dozen pedestrians.

"Blackfriars," said the cabby, pulling up and opening the trap over his passenger's head. "Did you want the bridge or the station?"

"Neither. Now take me to Charing Cross."

"What?" The cabby hesitated, and it was obvious that he wanted to know why his fare hadn't told him to go there in the first place, but all he said was, "Yes, guv'ner."

Closing the trap, he turned right and went west again, this time along the Embankment. The fog was thicker than ever here, so thick that they could barely make out the river to their left or the extended mass of the Temple on their right. Despite the lateness of the hour, there were enough lights on in the Savoy Hotel that they could see it as they went by. After they passed the Egyptian obelisk, which was called Cleopatra's Needle, the cabby again drew up and opened the overhead trap.

"Charing Cross," he said. This time he did not ask if his passenger wanted the railway station or the hotel, and he was not entirely surprised when Somerville said, "All right. Now take me to Westminster Bridge."

The note had given no reason for the complicated route he was to follow, but no explanation was needed. It was clear that somewhere along the way—perhaps in more than one place—someone was watching to make sure that he wasn't being followed.

The hansom went on up the Embankment, the subdued, yellow glow of the gaslights overhead marking the edge of the roadway, the place where the muddy waters of the river lapped against the granite retaining wall, and Somerville suddenly realized exactly where they were and wondered if there was any significance to it. For the stone and brick building to their right was one that had been much on his mind of late: Scotland Yard.

For the third time the cabby drew up.

"Westminster Bridge, guv'ner," he said. "Now what?"

"Go over it."

"Over the bridge?"

"Yes."

"I take it you know what you're about."

"I do."

"Righty-ho."

He turned the hansom and started across the bridge, the clop of the horse's hoofs sounding slightly hollow.

Somerville leaned forward, peering through the thick grey fog. Something was looming up ahead of them. As it came closer, he saw that it was what he had been looking for—a four-wheeler with one side light lit and one out. He immediately tapped on the overhead trapdoor.

"Driver, what time is it?"

"Dunno, guv'ner. Don't have no watch."

"Well, you should be able to see Big Ben from here."

"Strewth, you're right. Let's see." As soon as Somerville sensed that the cabby had turned to look up at the clock in the tower above the House of Parliament, he threw the Gladstone bag out so that it landed on the roadway near the opposite parapet.

"Looks like ten after one, guv'ner," said the cabby.

"Thank you," said Somerville.

He leaned out, looking back as the four-wheeler, which was going the other way, passed them by. It pulled up close to where the bag lay, and he saw the driver turn and stare after them, making sure that they were continuing on. Then, as the driver started to climb down from the box, a whip cracked over Somerville's head, the hansom swung around, and a police whistle shrilled piercingly once, twice, three times.

Climbing back into the box, the driver of the four-wheeler lashed his horse and sent it galloping toward the Parliament end of the bridge. The hansom drew up long enough for Somerville's cabby to jump down and pick up the Gladstone bag, then it went on again.

Dazed by what was happening, Somerville looked ahead. As the four-wheeler, going at a full gallop, reached the end of the bridge another four-wheeler appeared out of the fog and turned sideways, blocking the roadway. Instead of trying to stop, the driver of the galloping four-wheeler pulled on the reins and sent the growler up on to the sidewalk. There was a ripping, scraping sound as one side of it struck the back of the blocking four-wheeler, then it had brushed by and disappeared into the darkness.

The driver of the hansom swore softly overhead, then pulled up in front of the growler. A very large man in a helmet and cape stepped forward.

"I'm sorry, Inspector," he said. "He got away."

"Yes, I know, Sergeant. Not your fault."

Somerville got out of the hansom as the driver climbed down from his high seat, the Gladstone bag in his hand.

"Is that you, Inspector?" he asked.

"Yes," said Wyatt, unwinding the scarf from around his face. "I'm afraid we mucked it. I'm sorry."

"You should be," said Somerville in a flat, hopeless voice. "For by interfering as you did, you have ruined me and loosed something on London that is as bloody and dangerous as the Smithfield Slasher!"

At about that same moment Andrew sat up with a start. He had dozed off and was awakened by a low moaning. Pierre was twisting and turning, throwing himself from side to side. As Andrew put a hand on his forehead to quiet him, the door opened and Sara came in.

"I thought I heard something," she whispered. "Is he coming to?"

"I think so," said Andrew.

Pierre moaned again. Then suddenly he sat bolt upright in bed.

"*Le monstre!*" he groaned, his eyes wide with terror. "*Le monstre!*"

"Does that mean what I think it means?" asked Sara.

"Yes. The monster!"

10

The Somerville Secret

Wyatt led the way into the police station, opened the door to the small room he had been using as an office and let Somerville precede him into it. His face drawn, Somerville sat down heavily in the chair in front of the desk.

"Would you care for some tea?" asked Wyatt.

"I'd rather have a drink," said Somerville. "But since that's probably impossible at this hour . . . Yes, I'd like some tea."

Wyatt looked at Sergeant Tucker who nodded and went out, closing the door behind him.

"Do you want to begin now or would you rather wait until you've had your tea?"

"Begin what?"

"Don't you agree that you owe me an explanation?"

"I don't feel that I owe you anything!" said Somerville with a flash of temper.

"You do admit that you lied to me, misled me in several respects."

"Yes, I do admit that."

"Well, will you tell me the truth now?"

"About what?"

"About everything. Who the money in that bag was for, why you're paying it and what you meant by saying that I had ruined you and loosed something deadly on London."

"That certainly is everything," said Somerville heavily. "And even though it won't do any good, I suppose I should tell you the truth now. The question is where to begin."

"Would it help any if I told you I know a little about you, your family background?"

"Yes, it would. In that case, I'll begin with the first great change in my life—my marriage."

"I understand that it was a very good marriage."

"Good? It was a wonderful marriage. I'd known Louise for years. Her father, Lord Barham, was a friend of my father's, and I'd always been in love with her, had no idea she was the least bit interested in me, and could hardly believe it when she accepted me. My mother was dead by then, but my father was still alive and he was almost as happy about it as I was." He paused. "He was a very fortunate man. For when he died about three years later he knew we were going to have a child, and he was convinced that it was going to be a boy and that all was going to be well with the Randalls."

"Was he wrong?"

"Yes," said Somerville in a flat, uninflected voice. "He was wrong."

Sergeant Tucker came in with three mugs of tea on a tray, gave one to Somerville and one to the inspector. At the same time he gave him a note. Wyatt read it, glanced at Tucker, who had sat down in the corner with his notebook on his knee, and nodded. Somerville took a sip of his tea, then put the mug down and forgot about it.

"I was in London when the child was born. I wish I hadn't been, not that it would have made any difference in the end, but it wasn't my fault that I was away. I was to read a paper at the Royal Society; the doctor had told me that the child was not due for about two weeks, so I went. The next morning I got a telegram telling me to come back, but we had had a terrible snowstorm in the meantime, and it was another day before I was able to get home, back to Ansley Cross. By the time I got there, our child had been born, a son. Louise had him in her arms. She looked up at me, smiled, then—as if that was what she had been waiting for—she died."

"As a result of the delivery?"

"Yes. She was beautiful, intelligent, courageous, but not very strong. The doctor, Dr. Roberts, was a very good doctor, and he claimed he had done everything he could for her, but apparently it wasn't enough."

"That does happen occasionally."

"Yes. I won't try to tell you how I felt. Nothing meant anything to me anymore—nothing. Then I realized that that wasn't fair. Louise had wanted a child even more than I had, and had given her life to have him. So I must learn to love the boy no matter how I felt about him at the moment."

"You resented him?"

"Of course. I felt he was responsible for my wife's death. So I decided to go away until I could accept him as I knew I should."

"Where did you go?"

"To Mesopotamia—Tell Iswah. I had started a dig there several years before. As a matter of fact, Louise had been there with me for two seasons."

"Who took care of the child?"

"Mrs. Severn. She was a local girl and had done some upstairs work at Greyhurst, mending and so on. When Louise learned that her husband had been sent to jail and that she was going to have a child too, she promptly engaged her to make our child's layette, help out generally. She agreed to stay on, take care of the child and, as you know, she's with me still."

"Yes. What happened to her child?"

"Oh, it died a day or so before my son was born. We never discussed it; but in the light of the way she felt about Severn by that time, I don't think she was as sorry about it as she might have been."

"So you went to Mesopotamia. How long did you stay away?"

"For almost a year. When I came back, Mrs. Severn was . . . strange. She said the boy was fine, but there was something odd about the way she said it. I went up to see him and . . . at first I thought there was something wrong with me. That I couldn't accept him as I should because of what had happened to Louise. Then I looked at Mrs. Severn, saw the way she was looking at me, and realized that the child was not normal."

"What do you mean?"

"I'm not sure I can tell you. It's possible that no one can define the word normal exactly. But I knew—and I knew Mrs. Severn knew—that the boy was not like other children, either mentally or physically."

"Did you consult a doctor about him?"

"Not then. Dr. Roberts, who had delivered him and who would normally have taken care of him, had moved away. But a year or two later, when there was no longer any questions as to the fact that there was something wrong with him, I made an appointment under an assumed name with a doctor in Harley Street, and Mrs. Severn and I took him there."

"Why did you see him under an assumed name?"

"Because I did not want anyone—not even a doctor

one could presumably trust—to know that my son, the heir to a title that goes back six hundred years, was a monster."

"Was that what he was, a monster?"

"It's what he was becoming. The doctor said that he could not tell me why or how it had happened, but that occasionally these things *do* happen. The signs, he said, were very clear. The boy would never be normal and, as time went by, he would become even more abnormal—a creature of more than human size and strength, but of no intelligence, not even so much as an animal. On our way back to Greyhurst, I discussed the matter with Mrs. Severn. She was quite fond of the boy, was able to handle him without any trouble, and we made our plans."

"What were they?"

"I had let most of the staff go when I went away after my wife's death. Now I got rid of everyone else, except an elderly local woman to do the cooking and cleaning and a man to take care of the grounds. Mrs. Severn would take care of the boy, and if there were any inquiries—which was unlikely since I had been away so much that I had little to do with my neighbors—word was to be put out that the boy was not well and the doctors had left orders that he was not to have any visitors."

"When did you have those bars put on the windows of his quarters?"

"A few years later. Mrs. Severn said that he was always good, never threatening or dangerous, but I was afraid of what might happen if he got out and left the grounds."

"Did you see much of him during this time?"

"No. It was too painful, too disturbing. I deliberately kept away from him, staying in Paris when I was not in Baghdad or Tell Iswah. But a few years ago, even though no questions had been asked, I began to be afraid that some might be, so I decided to make a change. I took the place in London and when I went down to Greyhurst to get him and Mrs. Severn, I spread the word that I was taking him to school in Switzerland."

"That was how long ago—six years?"

"Yes."

"Before we get to the present, I can't help wondering why you went to all this expense, made these elaborate arrangements, when you could have done something very simple; put him in an institution somewhere, under another name if you liked, and say that he had died."

"But how could I?" asked Somerville in honest astonishment. "No matter how difficult taking care of him might be, it was not his fault that he was what he was. And he is my son."

"I see," said Wyatt, looking at him with approval as well as sympathy. "Very well. Go on."

"Well, as I said, I bought the house on Alder Road,

fixed a secure place there for him and, about a year ago, I engaged Sergeant Polk to act as custodian, watchman, bodyguard—whatever you choose to call him."

"Why did you feel that was necessary?"

"Because the boy was sixteen years old—as big and strong as a full grown man—and I was not sure Mrs. Severn could continue to handle him. Besides, after all his years in the army, I felt that Polk would be very useful in a crisis."

"You told him the truth—who the creature was?"

"Yes. Your father said I could trust him completely, and I did. Well, about a fortnight ago there *was* a crisis. Mrs. Severn's husband, Tom, suddenly appeared. She told you about that when you came to the house after Polk was killed."

"Yes. He wanted money and when she wouldn't give him any, he turned nasty and it was only when Polk came to the door and said he'd call the police that he left."

"That's right. Mrs. Severn knew him, knew how his mind worked, and had a feeling that she hadn't seen the last of him, so she sent me a telegram suggesting I'd better come here from Paris. But by the time I got here there'd been another incident—the watchdog I'd brought here from Greyhurst had been killed."

"I'm sure you know the reason for that now."

"I think so. Something—either Mrs. Severn's manner

or Polk's presence—gave Severn the feeling that she was hiding something, and he decided he'd get inside the house in some way and find out what it was."

"Exactly. He had a confederate named Gann who was a chimney sweep. He sent him around to solicit work and, when Mrs. Severn wouldn't let him in, he resorted to other methods. He poisoned your watchdog, and probably using a rope, climbed over the wall surrounding your grounds. Your son was in the small house in the garden?"

"Yes. I had had it specially built for him. Severn must have looked through the window, seen him and guessed who he was and why he was being kept there. Because the day after I got here I received a note saying that if I didn't want the world to know about the creature I had been hiding all this time, I should be prepared to come up with a thousand pounds. If I agreed, I was to lower the parlor curtains in a certain way."

"Was the note signed?"

"No."

"What did you do?"

"I was afraid that if I acceded to the demand, began to pay blackmail, there would be no end to it. So though I gave the signal that meant I agreed to the terms, I began making other plans."

"To take your son out of the country."

"Yes. I made the arrangements I described to you when you first came to see me. Polk rented a carriage and was to drive us to the coast. The reason we planned to leave at night was not because I was concerned about a chest of artifacts, but because we were transporting my son, who was heavily drugged."

"I suspected that you were not telling me the truth at the time. And I gather that someone else was suspicious of you, too."

"Yes. Severn, or whoever had sent me the blackmail note, must have been watching. When I went into the house, they killed Polk, pulled Mrs. Severn out of the carriage and made off with it, taking my son with them."

"I imagine you've heard from the kidnappers since."

"Yes. Twice. Two days after that, I got a note saying I apparently needed a lesson to prove that whoever was writing was not to be trifled with. I would get that lesson within the next day or so. And I did."

"That was the murder of the woman on Pentonville Road?"

"Yes. The cuff link that was found in her hand was Alfred's. He had been wearing it when he was kidnapped."

"What did the next note say?"

"It addressed itself to my deepest fears. Though Mrs. Severn had insisted that the boy was not dangerous, I had never been sure she was right, and I was afraid of what he might do if he got loose. He is sixteen years old now, as big and strong as a full-grown man, but with no intelligence—nothing to keep his appetites, his destructive drives in check. What they had done, these monsters who are far more monstrous than my poor boy, was to turn him loose and—for some reason—he killed the woman. The note now demanded not one, but two thousand pounds. If I agreed to pay it, instructions would be given to me as to how it was to be paid and the boy would be returned to me. If I refused to pay or if I went to the police, the boy would be turned loose completely, and what would happen after that, the death and destruction he would wreak, would be my responsibility."

"That was why you said what you did on Westminster Bridge."

"Yes."

"Do you have those notes?"

"No. In each case I was told to destroy them, and I did."

"Of course. Well, we'll have to see what we can do about the matter."

"But what can you do? Even if Severn is behind the whole thing, as seems probable, how can you find him—and find him before he turns that poor creature loose on an unsuspecting city?"

"As it happens, we know where Severn is. Or where he was a few days ago."

"You do know?"

"Yes. And that presents some problems. Because he was in an infirmary with a badly broken leg *before* Polk was killed and your boy kidnapped. Which means that it will be very hard to prove that he was involved. On the other hand, there may be another way to unravel the mystery." He glanced again at the note Tucker had given him when he came in with the tea. "Are they still here, sergeant?"

"I'm sure they are, sir. They said they'd wait."

"Good." Wyatt rose. "I suggest that you go home, m'lord. I'll be in touch with you as soon as I have something to report."

"Does that mean you think you may have something —some word—fairly soon?"

"I don't dare make any promises, especially after what happened tonight. We'll have to see."

"Thank you, Inspector." Somerville rose too, shook Wyatt's hand. "Even though it seemed impossible at the time, I'm beginning to think I might have been better off if I'd told you the truth, the whole terrible story, at the very beginning."

"I think it might have been better if you had. But we will see if, out of this nettle danger, we can't still salvage something."

He opened the door and followed Somerville out. Sara and Andrew, sitting on a bench against the far wall, stood up when they saw him.

"So you did wait," he said.

"Of course," said Sara. "Did the sergeant tell you why we came? That Pierre's conscious?"

"He told me. How long ago was this?"

"About three quarters of an hour ago."

"How did you get here?"

"Fred brought us. He's waiting outside."

"Good. We'll go back to the house with you. Come on, Sergeant."

11

Pierre's Story

In spite of the hour—it was well after three o'clock—the house on Rysdale Road was wide awake. Lights were on downstairs as well as upstairs, and when the landau drew up under the porte-cochere, Matson opened the front door.

"Shall I wait?" asked Fred.

"It's pretty late," said Andrew, "but perhaps you should."

"I was going to even if you said no."

"Why?"

"You know I like to be in on things; and when *he's* around," he nodded toward Wyatt, "there are usually things to be in on."

He shook the reins and drove the horses around the house and back toward the stable.

"Is he always like that?" asked Tucker.

"Usually," said Andrew. Then, as if that explained it, "He used to be a jockey." He led the way upstairs. "I don't think Matson likes the way he talks to me," he said, lowering his voice, "but there's nothing he can do about it because Fred's not just good with horses—he also makes my mother laugh. So that's that."

The door of the guest room was open. Pierre, with more color in his cheeks than he'd had before, was sitting up in bed and finishing a bowl of soup.

Mrs. Wiggins, wearing a nightcap and robe, was sitting next to him.

"Good evening, Inspector. Good evening, Sergeant," she said. "Or should I say good morning?"

"Good morning is certainly more accurate," said Wyatt. "How's our young friend?"

"He's a good deal better than he was. He was half starved along with whatever else that was wrong with him. This is his second bowl of soup."

"*Ça va, mon gar?*" asked Wyatt.

"*Oui, m'sieu,*" said Pierre somewhat shyly.

"This is the friend of whom I spoke," said Andrew in his simple, but understandable French. "He is an inspector in our police and you can trust him completely. He will see that no harm comes to you."

"Of that you can be sure," said Wyatt in extremely good French. "Would it be easier for you to tell us what we want to know in French than in English?"

"Yes, *m'sieu.*"

"Good. Then begin at the beginning and tell us your whole story—how you came to England and how you came to the house here the other night."

"Yes, *m'sieu*," said Pierre again, and he began his tale, pausing frequently to give Wyatt a chance to translate for Tucker, who was taking notes, and also of course for Sara.

He came from Marseilles, he told them. His father died when he was very young, leaving his mother, his brother and himself alone in the world. They were poor —his mother was a laundress—but they managed, especially when his brother became old enough to go to sea as a sailor and began to send them money. Then, about six months ago, his mother suddenly became sick, ran a high fever, and in three days was dead. His brother was away, so all at once he was completely alone, with no one to turn to.

"You had no other relatives?" Wyatt asked him.

Not in Marseilles, Pierre told him. His parents had come from further north, and although he believed they had relatives in Lyon, he did not know them. Neighbors helped him out for a few days, but they were even poorer than Pierre's family had been, and he did not like to take food from them. Each day he went down to the harbor to see if there was word of his brother, but he had shipped on a long voyage to the Far East and no one knew when he would return. Then, one day he met an English sailor—a bosun—who said he knew the brother, that he was in England and, if Pierre wanted, he would take him there."

"What did he say your brother was doing in England?" Wyatt asked.

"He said he had been hurt and was in hospital there. I was very happy. I went on to his ship with this man and worked hard in the galley and as cabin boy. The food was not good and the sailors laughed at me because I could not speak English, but I did not care. Soon I would be with my brother. But of course when we got to England my brother was not there."

"Had he been there?" Andrew asked.

"I think not," Pierre said. "The bosun said he had left the hospital and gone, but now I am sure he was lying, that he never knew my brother."

"But why did he say he did?" asked Sara.

"Because they needed a cabin boy—I found out later that the other one had run away—and me they did not have to pay. And besides, when we got to London, the bosun sold me to the cleaner of chimneys named Gann."

"Sold you?" said Sara, her eyes large. "How could he sell you?"

Pierre shrugged when Wyatt translated the question.

"They told me that I owed them money for bringing me from Marseilles to London, that M'sieur Gann had paid them the money and I must work for him till I paid him back."

"I've heard of such things," said Tucker. "If you can

get hold of a boy who doesn't speak English, then you not only don't have to pay him, but he can't complain, won't run away no matter what you make him do."

"I doubt if we can find the bosun, but I'm fairly sure we can find Matty Gann, go into this with him," said Wyatt grimly. "Go on," he told Pierre.

Gann took him to his place, a cellar room over there— Pierre pointed east—near the big railroad station that looked like a cathedral.

"St. Pancras," said Wyatt, and Pierre nodded.

There was another, older boy who worked with Gann, and together they began preparing Pierre for sweeping, rubbing him with a pickling solution and standing him in front of a fire to toughen him up so that he could crawl into flues that were still hot. It was a hard life, for when you were climbing one of the narrow chimneys you were half suffocated by the soot and when you came out your hands and knees were bleeding from the rough bricks. Most of the time he did not get enough to eat, but occasionally Gann and the other boy would go off at night and when they came home they would be in good spirits and there would be plenty of food, and Pierre would not have to work for several days.

"Probably doing a little breaking and entering," said Tucker. "A flue faker has a good chance to look a place over."

Pierre nodded. That's what he thought. Then Gann and the older boy quarreled, the boy left and things became so bad that Pierre was thinking of running away when suddenly a man appeared whom Gann apparently knew, a strange gypsyish man, and things changed again.

"Was his name Severn?" Wyatt asked him. "Sixty Severn?"

Yes, it was, Pierre told him. Shortly after Severn appeared, Gann and Pierre went to a house on Alder Road with a high wall around it and Gann tried hard to get the woman there to let him clean the chimneys. (This must have been the day that Wyatt and Andrew met Polk, Andrew decided later, for Pierre remembered seeing them as Andrew remembered seeing Pierre.)

When the woman said she did not want to have her chimneys cleaned, Gann and Severn brought Pierre back to the house that night and lifted him up so that he could look over the wall. There was a huge watchdog inside there that began growling and barking the moment it heard or smelled him, frightening him badly, but he had seen the small house in the garden and was able to describe it to Severn and Gann who seemed very interested in it.

Severn had them wait there for about an hour while he went away. When he came back, he had a piece of meat and some white powder with him. He sprinkled the powder on the meat and threw it over the wall. A few minutes later they picked Pierre up again and had him tie a rope to one of the iron spikes on top of the wall. While he was doing so he looked over the wall and saw the watchdog lying there. At the time, he didn't know if it had been drugged or poisoned, and that was all he did know then because, after he had tied the rope to the spike, Gann sent him home, and he didn't know what happened after that.

"Severn must have gone over the wall," said Tucker, "seen what was in the garden house, realized what his wife was hiding and why, and decided he could blackmail Somerville for a small fortune."

Wyatt nodded, told Pierre to go on.

The next morning Gann took Pierre back to Alder Road, apparently to find out what the results of the poisoning had been, determine whether anyone had seen them. It was while Gann was listening to Polk talk to the constable that the butcher boy had attacked Pierre, and he had been rescued by Sara and Andrew.

"It was the first time since I had been in England," he said, "that anyone seemed to care about me, that I felt I had a friend."

He looked at Sara and Andrew as he said this and, understanding what he meant even before Wyatt translated it, Sara smiled at him.

During the next few days Gann was away a good deal and Pierre saw very little of him. He remembered one night when Severn came for Gann and, as they were about to leave, Gann told Pierre that if he followed them, he'd kill him. It had never occurred to Pierre to follow him, and he didn't do so that night. But, once Gann had put the idea in his head, he thought about it and, a few nights later, he did follow him.

"When was this?" asked Wyatt. "How many days after the dog was killed was it that Gann told you not to follow him?"

About three days, Pierre told him.

"That would make it the night that Polk was killed and Somerville's son was kidnapped," said Tucker.

"Yes," said Wyatt. "And when did you follow him?" he asked Pierre.

About four days after that, Pierre told him.

"That's the night the woman was murdered on Pentonville Road," said Tucker.

"Yes," said Wyatt. "*Continuez, mon brave*," he said to Pierre.

Pierre hesitated, looked at Wyatt, then at Sara and Andrew.

"It's all right," Sara said, convinced that Pierre would understand her. "Andrew told you that you can trust the inspector and you can."

And of course he did understand. He nodded and went on.

Though they had cleaned a few chimneys since the night Gann had told him not to follow him, Gann had not been particularly interested in what they were doing and had seemed more and more tense and nervous. On this particular day he went out to a pub fairly early, came back with a bottle of gin, spent most of the afternoon drinking, then fell asleep. There was some stale bread and cheese in the cellar, and Pierre ate that for his supper. It was about eleven o'clock at night when Gann woke up. He did not seem to want anything to eat, which was probably a good thing because there was nothing, but he was upset when he examined the gin bottle and saw how little was left in it. He drank that, sat there muttering to himself for a while, then got up and went out without locking the door, which he usually did, and without saying anything to Pierre.

Without hesitating, Pierre went after him. He was not certain why he went, but he was quite sure that Gann was involved in something he shouldn't be, and he thought if he could find out what it was, it might help him to get free of Gann. In any case, he did go.

It was another foggy night, almost as foggy as tonight, he said, looking out of the window, and that made it easy for him to follow Gann, since he could keep quite close to him and Gann was too drunk to be concerned, to stop and look back.

They went north and east, past the big railroad station, then into an area of workshops and goods yards that was crisscrossed by stone and iron railroad bridges. There was no one else abroad there at that hour, and so even when Gann turned sharply one way or another, Pierre was always able to follow him by listening to the sound of his footsteps. On they went, past the huge black holding tanks of a gas works. The streets became even narrower, the brickyards and lumber yards gave way to tumbledown warehouses. Then Gann turned into an alley. Pierre went after him cautiously, and it was well that he did, for the alley led to the bank of a canal and, waiting there, was Severn. Pierre gathered that he had been waiting for Gann for some time—apparently Gann was quite late—and he was very angry. But he finally led Gann up the bank of the canal to a derelict, half-sunken barge. The bow was partly under water, but the cabin in the rear was still intact and, though the windows were covered with sacking, there were faint signs of light within.

Severn took Gann into the barge cabin, and a few minutes later came out alone and went striding off up the alley, passing within a few feet of where Pierre had hidden. Pierre remained there until the sound of Severn's footsteps had died away, then he stole up the canal bank to the barge. He stepped on to the deck and up to the cabin. There was no sound from within, and at first, because the window was covered, he could not see inside. But he went around to the other side of the cabin, and though the window there was covered with sacking too, it was not covered completely, and he was able to peer in through a crack.

He had been talking more and more slowly, his face getting more and more pinched and anxious.

"Gann was there," he said, Wyatt translating phrase by phrase. "He was sitting on a box with a club in his hand. And sitting on the other side of the cabin and staring at him was a monster."

Andrew had been expecting this. After all, the first words the French boy had said when he had recovered consciousness were *"Le monstre!"* But even so he felt a sudden chill of fear.

"What do you mean by a monster?" Wyatt asked him quietly. "Why do you call him a monster?"

Because that's what he was, Pierre told him. Though he looked like a man, was as big as Gann and perhaps bigger, he was not really a man. His forehead was low, his hair growing down almost to his eyes. His jaw was large and thrust forward like the muzzle of a beast, and through his parted lips his teeth looked like fangs. But it was his eyes that were more frightening than anything else. For, set deep under beetling brows, they were not only unblinking like those of the big cats, but somehow inhuman.

Pierre stared at the creature, who was watching Gann, then, in shocked horror, he backed away from the window. And that was his undoing.

One of the hawsers that held the barge to the dock was looped around the stern bitt and crossed the deck behind him. He tripped over it and fell with a thud. There was an exclamation from the cabin, the door burst open and, before he could scramble to his feet, Gann came out, the club in his hand.

"You!" he said, furious. Pierre wasn't sure what else

he said, probably something about the warning not to follow him; then picking him up by the front of his jacket, he struck him on the forehead with the club. As his knees buckled, Pierre felt himself lifted and thrown over the bulwarks of the barge into the canal.

It was Gann's haste and anger, Wyatt said later, that saved Pierre's life. For though he was unconscious from the blow on the head, the shock of the icy water brought him to. He was a good swimmer and, weak though he was, hardly aware of what he was doing, he swam to the end of the backwater in which the barge was moored. There was a ladder there and, after hanging on to it for several minutes, he was able to climb it and stagger out through the alley to the nearest street.

"How did he get here?" asked Sara.

"He's not really sure," said Wyatt after talking to Pierre. "He said he knew where you lived, knew that you were his only hope. He apparently stole a ride on a dray near one of the railroad yards, hooked another in back of a four-wheeler, and that took him close enough so that he could walk here."

"Well, I think he's a wonder!" said Sara. "How do you say that in French?"

"You don't have to," said Andrew. "He knows what you mean."

Pierre, pleased, smiled shyly and nodded.

"There's something else," said Tucker. "Something we should really be asking the doctor but, since he's not here . . . would you say he was well enough to get up, ma'am?" he asked Mrs. Wiggins.

"You mean now? Right now?"

"Yes, ma'am." He turned to Wyatt. "In the light of what happened the other night and what Lord Somerville told us this evening . . ."

"I agree," said Wyatt. "Every minute counts."

"Well, I'm not a doctor," said Mrs. Wiggins. "But if it's really important . . . yes, I think he could get up for a short while."

"The next question is one I'll have to ask Pierre," said Wyatt.

Pierre stared at him when he did, his eyes large and the color draining from his face.

"What did he ask him?" whispered Sara.

"If he thought he could find his way back there, to where he saw the monster," said Andrew. "And whether he'd take them there."

"*Je crois que je peux le trouver,*" said Pierre in a small voice. "*Mais j'ai peur. J'ai grand peur.*"

"He said, 'Yes. He thinks he can find the place, but . . .'"

"I know," said Sara. "He's afraid. And how can you blame him? He doesn't know the inspector as well as we do. On the other hand . . . Ask him if he'd feel better about it if we came, too."

"You come, too?" Pierre asked.

Sara and Andrew looked at Wyatt.

"If it will make him feel better about it," Wyatt said slowly, "I suppose you could come too."

"*C'est bon*," said Pierre. "Then . . . I go. I show you."

12

The Monster at Large

It took only a few minutes to get Pierre dressed. He was already wearing one of Andrew's pajama tops, and Andrew now gave him a shirt and jacket. They were both much too long—they came almost to Pierre's ankles —but they made it unnecessary for him to wear anything else. Though Matson had thrown out his old clothes, he had kept Pierre's cracked and battered boots and Pierre now put them on—not that he had any immediate need for them—for wrapping him in a blanket, Tucker carried him downstairs as if he were a babe in arms.

Fred, alerted by Mrs. Wiggins, was waiting outside the door with the landau.

"Pierre had better sit in the box so he can direct us," said Andrew. "I'll sit there with him."

Tucker lifted Pierre up into the box, and Andrew climbed up and sat next to him.

"Where to?" asked Fred when Sara, Wyatt and Tucker had climbed into the back.

"First stop is the police station," said Wyatt. "In the light of where we're going and what we may be up against, I want at least two more men with us."

"Righty-tight," said Fred, shaking the reins. He took the carriage out of the driveway, turned right on Rysdale Road, going up it at a fast trot, turned right again, and a few minutes later was drawing up in front of the police station.

"I want strong, reliable men," said Wyatt as Tucker jumped out. "And you'd better bring some extra glims."

Tucker nodded and hurried into the police station.

"Can we get two more men in here?" asked Sara.

"Yes," said Wyatt. And when Tucker reappeared, followed by two burly constables, he picked her up, sat her on his lap. "In here, men," he said.

"Now where?" asked Fred, as Tucker and his two companions climbed into the back of the landau.

"St. Pancras," said Wyatt. "Pierre will direct us when we get there."

"I take it you're in a bit of a hurry," said Fred, cluck-to the horses.

"We are."

"Hold on, then."

He turned the carriage, started down Wellington Road and began working his way east. The fog was not quite as heavy as it had been, but it was still so thick that the glow of the side lights carried only a few feet past the horses' heads. But that did not stop Fred. For all the sedate driving he had to do, there was nothing he liked better than clipping—and it wasn't often that he had a better reason for it than now with a Scotland Yard inspector telling him it was urgent. So by the time they approached Prince Albert Road, he had the horses in a fast trot, and once they were actually on the road, going past Primrose Hill, he put them into a gallop.

There was of course no one abroad at that hour, especially with London fogbound—no pedestrians, hansoms or vehicles of any sort—so there wasn't much danger of a collision. Their chief problem, it seemed to Andrew, was finding their way. But apparently that was no problem for Fred. Though he slowed down a little when they left the Regent's Park area and began driving through Camden Town, leaning forward and peering through the greyness, he still kept the horses at a fast trot. Before Andrew realized where they were, the huge bulk of St. Pancras station loomed up to their left, looking like a medieval cathedral with its ornate facades, arched windows, turrets and belfry.

"Now where?" Fred asked.

"*Par lá,*" said Pierre, pointing.

Fred turned left and began working his way through a maze of streets that were lined with storehouses, brick yards and lumber yards, with iron railroad bridges arching overhead like the webs of giant spiders.

"*Attendez,*" said Pierre finally. Then, as Fred slowed up, "*Oui. C'est lá,*" he said, pointing to a narrow alley between two tumbledown and abandoned warehouses.

"*Bon,*" said Wyatt, getting out of the landau.

"Shall I wait to make sure this is the right place?" asked Fred.

"You can if you want to," said Wyatt. "But . . ." He broke off as a scream—shrill, high, and in some curious way inhuman—sounded somewhere far off to their right. For a moment they all stood there frozen. Then, turning, Wyatt said, "Come on!" and went running up the alley, followed by Tucker and the two constables.

"Wait a minute," said Fred as Andrew jumped down off the box. "Where are you going?"

"After them," said Andrew. "You watch Pierre." And he and Sara went running up the alley after Wyatt and the policemen. The fog was thicker near the canal, the cobblestones underfoot were slippery and uneven, and twice, when the alley went off at an angle, they blundered into one of the walls. But finally they saw a faint gleam of light ahead of them, and a moment later they came out of the alley and into a very strange scene.

They were on the bank of a stagnant backwater of the Regent's canal. By the light of the bull's-eye lanterns that Tucker and the two constables carried, they could see the barge that Pierre had described, derelict and half sunk, with a ramshackle cabin at the stern. There was someone—a man—standing near the open door of the cabin. He turned as Wyatt and the constables approached the barge, and when he did, Sara and Andrew recognized him. It was the man many people near the Portobello Road called a saint.

"Is that you, Dr. Owen?" asked Wyatt, approaching the barge.

"Yes," said the doctor, leaning on his stick. He raised one hand to shield his eyes from the light of the lanterns. "Inspector Wyatt?"

"Yes."

"My compliments to you for finding your way here, but I'm afraid you're too late."

"Too late for what?" Then, seeing the body stretched out on the deck of the barge, "Who's that?"

"The man you were so interested in when you came to see me—Tom Severn."

"Is he dead?"

"Very."

By now Sara and Andrew were close enough to the barge so that they could see, not just the body, but the bloodstained hatchet that lay near it.

"Who killed him?" asked Wyatt.

The doctor looked at him thoughtfully. "How much do you know?" he asked.

"About what?"

"What Severn was up to. Who . . . or what he was keeping hidden here."

"If you mean Lord Somerville's son . . . Was that who killed him?"

"Yes."

"How? And why?"

Owen pointed to the bloodstained hatchet with his stick.

"There's the how. As to why . . . I only got here a minute or so ago, and by then it was all over—Severn was dead, and the poor mindless creature was gone; but . . . I think he killed Severn because Severn attacked him, hurt him in some way."

"Why do you say that?"

Again the doctor pointed, and by the light of the lanterns they saw a set of bloody footprints—the prints of large, bare feet—leading away into the darkness.

"Those prints were made with his own blood, not Severn's."

"How badly is he hurt?"

"I don't know. I told you he was gone by the time I got here."

"I have quite a few other questions to ask you, Doctor," said Wyatt coldly. "For instance, how a man with a broken leg—Severn—could have gotten about so spryly. How you got here, and how you know so much about what was going on. But in the meantime we're faced with a very dangerous situation."

"I agree. There's no telling what the creature may do next, whether he'll kill again."

"Exactly. My first task must be to go after him, capture him. But until then . . . can I have your word that you will remain here?"

"You cannot. I'm going with you."

"What?"

"I said I'm going with you. If you find the creature, he'll need treatment. He'll also need to be quieted down. I have the drugs to do that here." He held up his black bag.

Wyatt hesitated for only a minute. "All right," he said. Then he turned. "You!" he said to Sara and Andrew. "Back to the carriage, and have Fred take you home."

"But . . ." Sara began.

"Will you for once," said Wyatt angrily, "do what I say without an argument?"

"Yes, Inspector," said Andrew. Wyatt had never talked to them that way before, but then he had never been under such tension, never had so much reason to be anxious. "Come on, Sara."

They started toward the alley. When they reached it, they glanced back. Wyatt had taken one of the bull's-eye lanterns and, moving quickly, was following the trail of bloody footprints north towards the canal proper, followed by Tucker, the constables and the doctor.

"I don't think he should have talked to us that way," said Sara.

"He's worried, terribly anxious about what the creature might do."

"I know. And I don't really blame him. It's just . . . Well, you know how it is."

"Yes. You wanted to go along. So did I. But we can't always be in on everything."

"I suppose not."

They went back along the alley, stumbling on the slippery cobbles and feeling their way along the crumbling walls. When they came out into the narrow street, Fred was standing at the horses' heads and peering up the alley toward them.

"Well, that was a fine thing, going off like that," he said, trying to hide his relief. "What happened?"

"That shriek we heard was the monster," said Sara. "Severn hurt it; it killed him and went running off. Wyatt and the policemen have gone after it."

"What are we supposed to do in the meantime?"

"Go home."

"And about time too. Your poor friend here is shaking like he's got the ague." He lifted Pierre out of the box, wrapped the blanket more closely around him, and sat him in the back of the landau. "Sit there with him and try to keep him warm."

"Poor Pierre," said Sara, getting in and sitting down

next to him. "But I don't think he's cold. I think he's frightened."

"You are right," said Pierre. "I am frighten. *Le monstre est disparu?*"

"*Oui*," said Andrew. "*Il a été blessé et l'inspecteur le suive.*"

"*Ah, bon.* If he catch him, I feel better."

"The one good thing about all this," said Fred, turning the carriage, "is that your mother's away. Heaven only knows what she'd say about it if she were here with the two of you stravaiging about at all hours of the night like this!"

"You know very well what she'd say," said Andrew. "She likes the inspector, and she'd probably say, 'Good show!'"

"I shouldn't admit it," muttered Fred, "but you're probably right."

They were driving through the narrow streets behind St. Pancras station, under the stone arches and iron railroad bridges, and in spite of the fog that made it difficult to see more than ten or twelve feet ahead, Fred was guiding the horses with absolute assurance.

"Do you know where you're going?" asked Andrew.

"Why shouldn't I?"

"I just don't know how you can."

"Well, there's a lot you don't know. I'll lay you a bob I can tell you exactly where we'll be after we go under that next bridge there."

"Where?"

"St. Pancras Road."

"Done."

They went under the bridge, came out into a street that was much wider than the ones they'd been driving through.

"Well?" said Fred.

"I'm still not sure," began Andrew. He broke off as something flitted by under the horses' noses; they reared, whinnied and tried to bolt.

"Whoa there! Whoa!" said Fred, pulling them up. "What the devil was that?"

"I don't know, but it certainly scared them," said Andrew.

"Scared them? It gave them fits!" said Fred, trying to quiet the horses, which were still plunging and showing the whites of their eyes. "Do you think . . . ?"

"*Oui, oui, oui!*" said Pierre in a high, frightened voice. "*C'est le monstre!*"

Even as he said it, a whistle shrilled behind them, there was the sound of running footsteps and out of one of the narrow streets that they'd just left burst a group of men carrying bull's-eye lanterns.

"Blimey, but I think he's right!" said Fred. "There's the inspector and the coppers. Hoi!" he shouted, pointing to the left. "Tally-ho!"

"All right," panted Wyatt, running across the street toward them. "Hook it now! Off you go!"

"No, wait," said Sara as Fred lifted the reins and prepared to drive off.

"What?"

"I said, wait. Can't we wait just a minute and see what happens?"

"He said to hook it," said Fred. "And I think we should. But . . ."

He paused as Tucker and the two constables who had joined Wyatt all raised their bull's-eye lanterns and pointed them in the direction Fred had indicated. They were standing at the edge of an old cemetery, and the lantern beams moved slowly over the low white tombstones and occasional monuments. Suddenly one of the beams picked up a shape crouching in front of a white marble plinth. A second beam joined it, then the third—and all at once they could see him—or it. For by some trick of light, the three beams, meeting at one spot from three different angles, were reflected by the fog as if by a screen, and illuminated the hulking figure as if he had been standing on a stage.

Pierre moaned softly, Sara stiffened, and Andrew felt his blood run cold. It was not that he was huge—he was probably no taller than a tall man when he stood erect. And it was not that he was naked or hairy or oddly dressed for, though his feet were bare, he was wearing a white shirt and dark trousers. But it was precisely these quite ordinary elements, combined with his appearance and attitude—crouching there with his hands hanging well below his knees, low brow beetling, massive jaw projecting and deep-set eyes gleaming—that made him seem extraordinary . . . and frightening.

"Well, you wanted to see him," whispered Fred. "Now I hope you can forget him. I don't know if I can."

"He's a sight all right," said Tucker. "And he looks like he's ready for us, so what's the drill, Inspector?"

"I don't know," said Wyatt. "In spite of what happened, I don't know how dangerous he is. Can you tell us, Doctor?" he asked as, stick in one hand and black bag in the other, Dr. Owen came limping up to them.

"No," said Owen, breathing heavily. "I'm afraid I can't."

"Well, I can," said Sara in her clear, childish voice. "He's not dangerous at all. He's scared to death."

"Yes, he might very well be," said Wyatt. "But that's why . . ."

"That's why my eye!" said Sara, and before Andrew or anyone else realized what she was up to, she had jumped out of the carriage, brushed past Wyatt and the policemen and entered the cemetery, walking up through the gravestones toward the monster.

"Sara!" called Andrew.

"Come back!" ordered Wyatt.

Ignoring them, she went on. In the dead silence that followed—the only sound the shuffle of Sara's feet—Andrew suddenly realized that the creature was making faint mewing noises. And even as he identified the sound, he became aware that Sara, with her uncanny ear, was answering him—answering him with the same tone and in the same pitch as if they were both speaking the same language. Again the creature made a soft, mewing sound that was both plaintive and frightening—and again Sara responded, making soothing, repetitive sounds, much as a groom does when he's trying to soothe a fractious horse.

She had reached him now, and Andrew stopped breathing as she paused in front of the creature, small and slight in front of his crouching bulk. She looked down at his bare feet, one of which was covered with blood, and now she made another noise—still a noise, not words—but full of sorrow and sympathy. And now the creature answered her, repeating the sound that she had made, as if to say, "Yes. I hurt."

She reached up, took one of his hands; and then, with Sara leading him, they were walking together—the child and the creature—back through the graveyard to where Andrew and the others stood.

"All right," said Fred, speaking for all of them. "She's done it. And now I've seen everything."

13

The Truth at Last

It was a little before eight, not quite two hours later, when Wyatt rang the bell of the house on Alder Road. Lord Somerville, wearing the same tweeds he had been wearing the night before, opened the door.

"Oh, Inspector. You said you'd be back, but I didn't know when."

"Neither did I. My young friends are still here?"

"Yes. And the sergeant. In here." He led the way into the parlor. "We've been having some breakfast."

"Good." Wyatt looked at Tucker, who was sitting next to the door, then at Sara and Andrew on the far side of the room with a tray between them. "Where are Mrs. Severn and the doctor?" he asked Somerville.

"With Alfred. The poor creature was hurt, you know."

"Yes, I know. Would you get them, please?"

Somerville nodded and went out.

"All's well here," said Tucker when Wyatt looked at him inquiringly.

"Where were you?" asked Sara.

"Here and there," said Wyatt. "You shouldn't ask questions like that."

"I know that if you don't want to answer, you won't."

"Thanks for letting us stay here," said Andrew.

"It seemed only fair after what the two of you did. Fred took Pierre back to your house?"

"Yes," said Sara. "We told him to tell Mum we'd be home soon."

"You can go right now," said Wyatt, smiling faintly.

"Before we find out what we want to know? Thanks!"

The door opened, and Mrs. Severn came in, followed by Dr. Owen and Lord Somerville.

"How is he?" asked Wyatt.

"All right," said the doctor, setting down his bag. "I bandaged his foot and was prepared to give him some laudanum to quiet him down, but it wasn't necessary. He's asleep." He turned to Sara. "May I say that what you did there in the cemetery was one of the most remarkable things I've ever seen?"

"It was nothing," said Sara, blushing a little.

"I don't agree."

"Neither do I," said Somerville. "I've thanked our young friend once already and shall do so again—more concretely—when we've finished our business here."

"I suppose we'd better get on to that," said the doctor straightforwardly. "You had some questions you wanted to ask me, didn't you?" he said to Wyatt.

"I did. But there's something I'd like to ask Lord Somerville first. When we first arrived back here with your son, you looked at Dr. Owen rather strangely. Would you tell me why?"

"Because . . . Of course it's a good many years now and he doesn't look the same, but . . . he reminded me of someone."

"Of whom?"

"Of Dr. Roberts."

"Who is Dr. Roberts?"

"A doctor down at Ansley Cross, the doctor who took care of my wife, delivered my son."

"Did he remind you of Dr. Roberts too, Mrs. Severn?" asked Wyatt, turning to Somerville's housekeeper.

"There's no need for her to answer that," said the doctor. "I am Roberts."

"Would you mind telling us why you've been practicing medicine here in London under the name of Owen?"

"I'll try. My reasons were complicated and perhaps not entirely estimable. Do you know anything about my background, what happened at Ansley Cross?"

"I know a little."

"I thought you did. A few months before Lord Somerville's son was born, my wife left me. It was a bad blow, and I'm afraid I didn't take it very well. I began to drink. Lord Somerville wasn't aware of it. He and his wife were my most important patients, and I was particularly careful to be discreet when I was to see either one of them. But other people became aware of it, and my practice began to suffer. Then, shortly after the Somerville child was born, I had an accident. My carriage turned over, and both my legs were broken. I was told that they were never going to heal properly and, as you can see, they never did. I knew it was going to be difficult for me to practice in the country, so I sold out and came to London."

"Why did you take the name of Owen?"

"Because I had a great many debts I was afraid I would not be able to pay," said the doctor somewhat shamefacedly. "So I thought I would just drop out of sight."

"By spreading the story that you were leaving the country."

"Yes."

"Instead, you came here to London, opened an office and infirmary."

"Not right away. I wasn't even sure I wanted to practice medicine anymore at first. I took rooms near Portobello Road. Then, when I saw the need of the people in the area, I opened an office under the name of a friend with whom I'd been to medical school and who had died. Then, a few years later, I opened the dispensary and infirmary."

"After I saw you the other day, I asked Sergeant Tucker to do some investigating. Would you repeat what you told me, Sergeant?" he said.

"Yes, Inspector," said Tucker. "The report was rather mixed. There's no question but that the doctor is highly regarded in the area and has done a great deal of good work, often without a fee. At the same time I got the impression that he has sometimes performed illegal operations and treated suspicious wounds without informing the police as he is required to do."

"Any comment, doctor?" said Wyatt.

"Are you charging me with any of the things the sergeant mentioned?"

"No. But I would like to ask you a question. Or rather, several questions. The first one is, how could Tom Severn—or Sixty as he was usually known—have gotten about as he seems to have done if his leg was broken?"

"He couldn't," said the doctor promptly.

"What does that mean?"

"His leg wasn't broken."

"But you said it was, showed me the time he was admitted in your admissions register."

"I know. I lied and falsified the entry."

"Why?"

"Severn was a dangerous man. He told me he needed an alibi, didn't tell me why until I'd agreed to give him one. Then he told me that if I split on him, didn't continue to cover for him, he'd kill me."

"Do you think he would have?"

"Yes, I do."

"If what you say now is true, then Severn could have been—probably was—one of the men who killed Sergeant Polk outside here the night that Lord Somerville's son was kidnapped."

"That's correct."

"Had you known Severn before this—before he asked you for an alibi?"

"Yes. I knew him down at Ansley Cross before he was sent to Dartmoor. Then I saw him again a few months ago after he came back from Australia."

"Where?"

"At the dispensary. He turned up with a bad knife wound on his face. I recognized him at once, didn't say anything to him but, after he'd stared at me for a while, he apparently recognized me."

"Did he want to know why you were calling yourself Owen when your name was really Roberts?"

"Yes."

"What did you tell him?"

"The truth—that I had debts I could not pay, wanted to drop out of sight and start over."

"Is that another reason you agreed to lie, give him an alibi?"

"Yes. He said he was sure I had even better reasons than the ones I had given him for changing my name, wouldn't want him to start telling people who I really was."

Wyatt nodded. "I think he was one of those people who find blackmail emotionally satisfying as well as financially rewarding."

"I agree with you. I think the sense of power it gave him—especially over those he considered his superiors—was very important to him."

"Now we come to Lord Somerville's son. Did you know about him, see him or have anything to do with him before tonight?"

"Yes, I did."

"When and how?"

"I first saw him a little over a week ago, the night—at least, I gather it was the night—that Severn kidnapped him. He—Severn, I mean—woke me, said there was someone I had to look at, take care of."

"Somerville's son?"

"Yes. Of course, I didn't know who he was at the time."

"Where was this? At the barge?"

"Yes. The poor creature was in a bad way. Severn had him tied up, and he was struggling with the ropes, making those pathetic sounds, and Severn was afraid he'd do himself a mischief."

"What did you do?"

"I gave him some laudanum to quiet him down, left some with Severn to give him later on if he needed it."

"You say you didn't know who he was. Didn't you ask Severn about him?"

"Yes. He said he was a natural, a poor backward creature that he was taking care of for a while for a friend."

"Did you believe him?"

"Not really. I knew he was up to something—I didn't know what—but I didn't want to press him on it. As I told you, I knew he was a dangerous man and during the years I've been in London I've discovered it's sometimes best not to know things, not to ask questions."

"And what about before you came to London?"

The doctor looked at him, puzzled and a little startled.

"What do you mean?"

"You were the Somervilles' physician, took care of Lady Somerville during her pregnancy, did you not?"

"I did."

"And you delivered her child when he was born?"

For the first time the doctor hesitated.

"No," he said finally. "I did not deliver him."

"How did that happen?"

"There had been a bad snow storm—the worst in years. It took some time for one of the footmen to get through to tell me I was needed. By the time I got to Greyhurst, the child had already been born."

"I see. Mrs. Severn delivered it?"

"Yes."

"When you saw him did he seem well and healthy?"

Again the doctor hesitated.

"I asked you a question, Doctor. If you'd rather not answer it, would you answer another one for me. Why was Tom Severn called Sixty?"

"Forgive me, Inspector," said Somerville. "I'm sure you have some reason for asking these particular questions, but I must confess it escapes me. Do they relate in any way to any of the things that have been happening recently?"

"Why, yes, m'lord. I think they do. Don't you, Mrs. Severn?"

Mrs. Severn's face, always rather pale, was paler than ever now—pale and strained.

"Yes," she said.

"Can *you* tell us why your husband was called Sixty?"

Her dark and troubled eyes were fixed on Wyatt's face, clearly trying to decide just how much he knew. Finally she made up her mind.

"Yes," she said. "Not many people called him that—Tom didn't like it—and even fewer people knew where it came from, but . . . it was short for Six Toes. Because that's what he had, six toes on each foot instead of five."

"Right," said Wyatt. "An anomaly more common among animals than humans, but still far from unknown. Correct, Doctor?"

"I've only known one other case in all the years I've been practicing, but in general . . . yes."

"Then it was you who delivered Lady Somerville's baby, Mrs. Severn?"

"Yes."

"To repeat the question I asked Dr. Roberts, was it well and healthy when it was born?"

"No," she said, speaking with an effort. "It wasn't."

"What was wrong with it?"

"I don't know what was wrong, but . . . it was born dead."

"What?" said Somerville. "What did you say?"

"Please let me continue," said Wyatt. "When I have finished, you can ask all the questions you wish."

"But did you hear what she said? And do you realize what it means?"

"Yes," said Wyatt firmly. "Now will you please be patient?"

His face working, reflecting shock and incredulity, Somerville looked at him. Then with great effort, he controlled himself.

"Very well," he said in a strained voice.

"Go on, Mrs. Severn. You say Lady Somerville's child was born dead."

"Yes."

"Will you tell us what happened?"

"Dr. Roberts arrived at Greyhurst about a half hour

later. I told him what had happened, and he looked at the child, said he had been worried about it *and* about Lady Somerville. She had had a very hard time and was unconscious at the moment, and he said he didn't think she was going to live either. Suddenly she opened her eyes, began whispering that she wanted her baby. Dr. Roberts said he couldn't tell her the child was dead, didn't know what to do. But I said I knew, and I did it."

"What did you do?"

"My baby had been born two days before, shortly after Lord Somerville left for London. I got him and gave him to Lady Somerville to hold."

"Why?"

"I thought, if she was going to die, at least she would die happy. And it did make a difference. She quieted down, began smiling, and Dr. Roberts looked at me and nodded as if he thought I had done the right thing."

"True, doctor?" asked Wyatt.

"Yes."

"Go on, Mrs. Severn."

"About an hour later Lord Somerville came home. My lady was still holding the baby. She looked up at him and smiled . . . and died. Lord Somerville told me to take the baby away so he could be alone with her, and I did. Then, about an hour later, he came out and asked me if I would stay on and take care of the baby for him—and I suddenly realized he thought the child was his."

"You had not intended this—to pass your child off as his—to begin with?"

"Of course not. He was my child, and I loved him. I told you why I gave him to Lady Somerville to hold. But once Lord Somerville accepted him as his, I saw what it could mean. He could be my son and Tom's—a jailbird's son—and not only have nothing, but be marked for life or he could be Lord Somerville's son and have everything—a title, wealth and a father who loved him and would take care of him. It didn't take me long to decide what to do."

"Which was to say nothing, let Lord Somerville go on thinking the child was his."

"Yes."

"What did you plan to do about Dr. Roberts who knew the truth?"

"I thought I'd talk to him, tell him why I was doing it and ask him not to say anything about it. But I didn't have to. Because a day or so later he had that accident, was in hospital for several weeks and then left Ansley Cross for good."

"What happened to the dead child—Lord Somerville's son?"

"After he'd talked to me, asked me if I'd take care of his son, he noticed that I looked different and asked me what had happened with my child. I . . . I told him it had been born dead, and he said he was sorry and that I should bury him in the Randall cemetery."

"Which you did. And so that is where he lies now, under the name of Severn."

"Yes."

"When did you discover that there was something wrong with the boy?"

"Quite a bit later. I thought he was just a little slow at first, and Lord Somerville was away most of the time —he didn't really want to see the child because he felt he was responsible for Lady Somerville's death. But when he did see him he got worried, and we took him down to London to see a doctor on Harley Street and he said . . ."

"Lord Somerville told me what he said."

Somerville looked at Mrs. Severn without really seeing her.

"All these years," he said. "Lost and empty years when I could not bring myself to come back to England because England meant *him*—what I thought of as my secret and my curse." His eyes focused. "I still don't see how you could have done it, Mrs. Severn. Done it to me, I mean."

"I told you how it began," she said, speaking slowly, painfully. "Then afterwards, when I discovered that he wasn't right in the head, I . . . well, it became harder than ever to tell you the truth. Because if people knew he was my son, they would have put him away. But as it was, with you thinking he was yours, I could be with him, take care of him."

"I often wondered why he meant so much to you—more than he did to me. Not that it's hard to understand my feelings. Because I did resent him, partly because I felt he was responsible for my wife's death—and partly because of what he was—or rather, wasn't; someone to whom I could never pass on the title. Did Severn know the truth—that the creature was his own son?"

"I don't think so," said Mrs. Severn. "He certainly didn't find out from me."

"I don't think he knew either," said Wyatt. "At least, not until the very last minute. Then . . . well, it's because of what he did when he did find out that he died himself."

"What do you mean?" asked Somerville.

"Severn was not working alone. He had a chimney sweep named Matty Gann working with him. I don't know what else they did—I suspect that they were involved in quite a few robberies—but I know that Gann was here with Severn the night of the kidnapping, the night that Polk was killed."

"How do you know that?" asked Somerville.

"I had testimony to that effect from a climbing boy who worked with Gann—someone my friends here found for me." He nodded toward Sara and Andrew. "And now I have additional confirmation from Gann himself."

"You've got Gann?" asked Sara.

"Yes. We've been looking for him for several days,

picked him up early this morning. He was hurt, slashed by Severn, but not so badly hurt that he couldn't talk, confirm some things I suspected."

"Do they relate to what you said before?" asked Somerville. "That it was finding out that the creature he thought was my son was his own that led to his death?"

"Yes," said Wyatt. "Gann guarded the boy last night on the barge where they'd been hiding him, keeping him prisoner, while Severn was out trying to collect the backmail money he'd demanded of you. When Severn got back, in a rage because he hadn't gotten the money, Gann made the mistake of pointing out something that Severn had never noticed before—that the creature had six toes on each foot just like Severn. In that moment, Severn must have realized what it meant. That the creature was not your son, but his own. More furious than ever, he attacked Gann, driving him away because he immediately saw something else—that if you knew the truth—that Alfred wasn't your son—you wouldn't be willing to pay Severn to keep quiet about him and return him to you. And since he evidently intended to make another attempt to blackmail you, and didn't want you to find out what he'd just discovered himself, he did something as cold-bloodedly vicious as anything I've ever heard of."

"What was that?" asked Somerville.

"I know!" said Sara with fascinated horror. "He tried to cut off those extra toes—the sixth ones!"

"Exactly," said Wyatt. "He thought that by doing that, he'd be able to keep you from making the connection he had made, guessing the truth."

"Oh, no!" said Somerville. "He couldn't do that! Not to his own flesh and blood!"

"Yes, he could," said Mrs. Severn harshly. "You never said so, but I know you always thought of Alfred as a monster. But it was *he* who was the real monster—Tom!"

"I agree," said Wyatt. He turned to the doctor who had been listening intently. "You said that Severn was dead and the creature was gone by the time you got to the barge."

"That's correct."

"Why had you gone there?"

"Severn had sent me a message asking me to come. I suspect he thought he might have trouble with the creature again, wanted me to give him something to quiet him if it should prove necessary."

"Did he tell you to bring your bag with you?"

"No, he didn't. But I brought it anyway—I always do."

Wyatt nodded. "May I look at it for a moment?"

"Of course." The doctor handed him his black leather bag. Wyatt hefted it as if judging its weight, opened it and glanced inside it, then handed it back.

"Thank you," he said. "Will you tell us what you think happened before you got to the barge?"

"I'm a doctor, not a detective," said Roberts, "and I didn't realize the significance of the six toes until you pointed it out just now, but I suspect that what you suggested was true. Severn cut off one of the creature's toes, and the creature, shocked and terrified because it had never been hurt before, took the hatchet away from Severn, killed him with it and then ran off."

"Yes," said Wyatt. "That's what I thought you meant."

"No!" said Mrs. Severn. "Alfred wouldn't do that! He couldn't do that!"

"Does that mean that he's going to be charged with murder?" asked Somerville. "Since he was attacked, I should think it could be called self-defense. And besides, can someone with his mentality—or lack of it—be held accountable for his actions?"

"I'm inclined to doubt it," said Wyatt. "But there's another, even more cogent reason why I don't intend to charge him. Did you examine Severn's body when you got to the barge?" he asked Roberts.

"No, I didn't. I didn't have time before you came."

"Then you don't know what the cause of death was."

"Not really. But since his head was bloody and there was blood on the hatchet, I assumed that that was the weapon, and that he was hit on the head with it."

Wyatt nodded. "That's what did happen. That's how he was killed. However, the wound was in a very interesting place. In the *back* of Severn's head."

"I don't think there's anything startling or surprising about that," said the doctor. "If things happened as we suspected—if the creature took the hatchet away from Severn—isn't it likely that Severn turned to run away? That would make it possible for the creature to strike him in the back of the head."

"Yes, it would," said Wyatt. "There is, however, another interesting fact. The creature, for all his limited mental capacity, is right-handed. I noticed it when Sara led him from the cemetery, and I saw him use his right hand in preference to his left several times when we were bringing him here. The wound that killed Severn, however, was on the *left* side of the back of his head and could only have been dealt him by . . ."

With surprising speed, the doctor leaped to his feet and raised his heavy cane to strike at Wyatt. But quick as he was, Andrew was just as quick. Almost as if he had been anticipating it, he jumped up and grabbed the end of the cane. Turning with an oath, the doctor pulled it away from him and raised it again—but by this time Sergeant Tucker had crossed the room and, clamping a large hand on the cane, took it away from him.

"Now, now, Doctor," he said mildly. "Let's not have any of that."

"I was going to say," said Wyatt, "that Severn could only have been killed by a left-handed man—like you, Doctor."

"You mean it was *he* who killed Severn, not Alfred?" asked Somerville.

"Yes."

"But why?"

"I think that most of what he told us concerning his life before he came to London was the truth. I think he even told the truth about the reason for changing his name. But I think that his practice during these past few years has been more questionable than appeared at first. Not that he hasn't done a great deal of charity work, which made him highly regarded. But along with his good works—which were a useful front—there was a good deal of another kind that was extremely lucrative. When Severn came to see him to have the slash on his face taken care of, they not only recognized one another— they also recognized that they were both of the same stripe and could be useful to one another. Severn, just back from Australia, saw at once that the doctor's knowledge of the underworld could be a help to him. He undoubtedly consulted with the doctor when he became curious about what his wife was doing in London, what she was hiding; and it was probably from the good doctor that he got the poison he used to kill the watch-dog. True, doctor?"

The doctor, sitting again, with Tucker standing immediately behind him, looked up with hooded eyes but did not answer.

"While our friend here must have been surprised to

hear that Lord Somerville had an heir, he undoubtedly guessed the truth; but I doubt that he told Severn that the creature was *his* son, not yours, my lord. My guess is that he helped plan the various steps that followed: the first blackmail letter, the kidnapping of Alfred, and the final arrangement for payment that we blocked. When he came to the barge, and discovered that the plan had not only failed but that Severn by hurting the creature had driven it to escape, he picked up the hatchet and killed Severn. He did this, not in anger—though he undoubtedly was angry—but because if he could find Alfred and continue with the blackmail scheme, he would not have to share the proceeds with Severn. And if he could *not* find Alfred again and had to abandon the scheme, he had silenced the only possible witness to his involvement. And, of course, he could blame the death on Alfred. Again I ask you, is that correct, Doctor?"

"Do you really expect me to answer that?"

"No, Doctor. I don't expect you to say anything. And since that's so, there's no need to keep you here. Sergeant, will you take him to the station house? I'll be along shortly to make out the charge."

"Yes, Inspector," said Tucker. "Come along, Doctor." And holding him firmly by the arm, he led him from the room.

"I'm overwhelmed," said Somerville. "Too many things have been happening too quickly for me to even begin to understand them. The poor creature I had thought of as my son turns out not to be—and Dr. Roberts, whom I had begun to feel was as much a victim as I was, turns out to be even more of a monster than Severn. But when did you first suspect him?"

"When I first met him. Because I was convinced that Severn had a great deal to do with Polk's death, and it seemed very strange that he had such a perfect alibi. But apparently I wasn't the only one who suspected him. You were on him like a pouncing hawk when you grabbed his cane," he said to Andrew. "Did you suspect him, too?"

"No," said Andrew.

"Then what made you react so quickly?"

"I don't know." He thought a minute. "Yes, I do. I knew you must have had some reason for asking him to let you see his bag, but I didn't know what it was until you started talking about Severn's wound—and then I suddenly realized that when he handed you the bag, it was with his left hand."

"Good for you!" said Wyatt. "I seemed to remember that he was left-handed from our visit to his nursing home, but I wanted to make sure."

"What will happen to him?" asked Sara.

"I've little doubt that he'll be found guilty. As to what his sentence will be, that's something else and, in a sense, no concern of mine."

"And Alfred?" asked Mrs. Severn. "What will become of him now?"

"I think, in the light of what's happened," said Somerville, "that you should no longer try to take care of him yourself."

"I know," she said. "I've been fair sick these last days when he was gone, thinking of what he might do or what might happen to him. But . . . what kind of a place will they put him in?"

"It need not be a public institution," said Somerville. "Though I understand that some of them are quite good. We will find the best possible place for him, and I will take care of the expense."

She stared at him. "But why should you do that after what I did—the way I deceived you?"

"Perhaps because, after having felt responsible for him all these years, I find it difficult to stop. Perhaps because I believed you when you said you did what you did out of love, concern for the poor creature. But mostly because—terrible, difficult and lonely as these years have been—they are over now, and I am not too old to think of the future; a future I don't think my dear Louise would have resented."

"I take it there is someone in whom you are interested," said Wyatt.

"Yes. I met her in Paris, have loved her for years. With my dark and awful secret always on my mind, I could not speak to her—for how could I be sure that if I had another child he would not turn out like Alfred? But now . . . I shall leave for Paris as soon as possible—

probably tomorrow, and . . ." He broke off as Sara leaned over and whispered in Andrew's ear, and Andrew frowned at her, shaking his head. "Is anything wrong?" he asked.

"No, sir," said Andrew.

"Are you sure? I'm greatly in your debt—Miss Wiggins's especially—for everything you did, the way you helped resolve all this. And if there's anything I can do to show my gratitude and appreciation . . ."

"There's no need for you to do that, sir."

"I agree," said Wyatt. "We can handle this particular matter by ourselves without troubling you."

"You mean you know what Miss Wiggins was talking to our young friend about?"

"I believe so. I know that she's been quite concerned about Pierre, the young French boy, anxious to help him find his brother. And since you were going to France anyway, she thought . . ."

"How did you know that?" asked Sara, staring.

"If a detective is to be successful, he must understand how a criminal's mind works. And if he can do that, he should certainly know how a colleague's mind works. Especially," and he bowed, "a colleague with whom he has had such a long and rewarding association."

"Oh, coo!" she muttered, coloring. "If you're not a blarneying barney I don't know who is!"